M000031788

More Short Stories for Long Rainy Days

More Short Stories for Long Rainy Days

SIMPLE TALES OF LIFE AND LOVE

KATHERINE ANNE DOUGLAS

PROMISE
PRESS
An Imprint of Barbour Publishing

Acknowledgements

The author is grateful to everyone at Barbour Publishing who had a part in this work. She is thankful as well for her friends, family, and colleagues whose enthusiastic response to her first book made this second one possible. Thank you all!

ISBN 1-57748-572-6

Published by Promise Press, an imprint of Barbour Publishing, Inc., P.O. Box 719, Uhrichsville, Ohio 44683, http://www.barbourbooks.com

 Member of the
Evangelical Christian
Publishers Association

Printed in the United States of America.

Dedication

This book is dedicated to family and friends
who unknowingly contributed to it.

Contents

Preface

Some people have absolutely no use for fiction. They find this made-up, manufactured, daydreamy entertainment a mindless expenditure of time and resources. "It is not *fact*," they say. "It is not *real*."

I don't know if the Lord Jesus Christ enjoyed reading made-up stories, but He obviously enjoyed *telling* them. Back then they were called "parables." The Bible tells us that Jesus "taught (people) many things by parables" (Mark 4:2). Another Scripture says that the Lord Jesus "did not say anything to them without using a parable" (Matthew 13:34). We're also told He had a few different reasons for His use of fiction, but I'll let you discover those for yourself.

For now, however, take a few minutes to set aside the *factual* manual or textbook you *will* have to read sooner or later. Relax and enjoy a "made-up" story or two. Like the parables of Jesus, these are written to do more than entertain. I hope you enjoy them.

Katherine Anne Douglas

CHAPTER 1

Second Thoughts

Let him who walks in the dark, who has no light,
trust in the name of the LORD and rely on his God.
—Isaiah 50:10 NIV

Andrea Sanderson resisted the impulse to pace the floor. She thought of washing the crystal in the dining room hutch, but one look at the enormity of the task convinced her to find something else to busy her hands. Perhaps this restlessness was related to what she was sure was her approaching menopause. She looked out the window once again for her husband, Blake, to saunter into the driveway, whistling and dripping wet from his morning run. She smiled. How did she ever get mixed up with this fitness freak? She didn't have an athletic bone in her body! Her smile faded with the thought. How, indeed, did she get "mixed up" with the wonderful man whom she lovingly and proudly called her husband? She suddenly realized why she was so ill at ease, why she had slept so fitfully the night before.

Second thoughts. Doubts. Dark suspicions hovered at the back of her mind, clamoring for attention. She thought she was long past them, that she had outgrown them. She thought she had prayed them away. She thought Blake had succeeded in convincing her that they were foolish and unfounded. She thought she was done with them. Apparently not. She went outside and sat on the wicker swing on the porch. She bowed her head.

"Holy Father," she prayed, "help me to trust You. Help me to trust Blake."

She could not pray beyond that. She had forgotten how powerful these paralyzing suspicions could be. Why should they come now? What had prompted the return of these insidious monsters, giving her that dreaded feeling in the pit of her stomach? That discomfort promising the arrival of a gnawing headache? Ten years! It had been ten years since she had had doubts about Blake, or about herself—she wasn't sure which they were.

Like it had been yesterday, she remembered her first date with Blake. She had dated little in her lifetime and she was thirty-eight when Blake asked her out. She could hardly believe her ears! Blake Sanderson wanted to go out with her? She had looked around the break room at work to make sure someone hadn't put him up to it on a dare. She was not the most attractive woman in the department and she certainly wasn't the only single woman. Blake was new to the company. He was the only single man in the department and most certainly the most attractive. Andrea remembered being so shocked by his invitation that her response was totally without grace or even common courtesy.

"Me? You want to go out with me?" she had asked, dumbfounded.

"Someone said you know your way around Columbus better than anyone. I thought it would be a good opportunity for us to get to know one another better! You could show me places to go and things to do! Besides, you were the only one in the office to invite me to your church, so I figure you won't take me to any places that my mother wouldn't approve."

She had looked at him with no small amount of disbelief and saw he was teasing. She had blushed and relaxed in the same moment. "Well, sure, Blake. I'd love to show you around your new hometown," she had said, recovering her equilibrium.

In the course of their first date, which had begun perfectly, Andrea learned something about Blake that unsettled her. His age. Blake was ten years younger than she. He had not registered any surprise when she told him her age. He had barely acknowledged it. He had continued to ask her question after question on their whirlwind tour of the city sights and, admittedly, it had been one of the most wonderful evenings of her life.

After their third or fourth date, Andrea had decided she had better stop their relationship from deepening into anything more than a friendship. She was enjoying Blake's company far too much than was safe, to her way of thinking. She saw him at the office. She saw him at church. He invited her to lunch often enough that her friends at work had started asking pointed questions. And her attraction to him was growing so fast she had found herself wondering what she ever did before Blake Sanderson showed up on the threshold of her office cubicle and her life.

She had made her decision. Yet she kept saying "yes" whenever he asked her out. After six months they were an "item" at the office. After nine months she was hopelessly in love. And miserable. A year after their first date, Blake proposed. She had burst into tears as he had opened the small jewelry box and asked her to marry him.

"This was not the response I expected!" He laughed and pulled her into his embrace.

"It. . .it won't work, Blake. I know it won't," she blubbered.

"Hey! What is this, Andi? I thought these were tears of

joy!" He lifted her chin. His smile had disappeared.

"What won't work? Us? You're kidding, right? We've been 'working' for over a year now!"

She gently freed herself from him and went for a tissue. He stood quietly, waiting for her explanation. It had taken her ten minutes to compose herself enough to speak. Blake stood quietly the entire time.

"I knew I should have ended this before it began. But I didn't, and here you are proposing marriage to me!" Her tears threatened again and she took a deep breath.

"When two people love each other, this is usually what they do, Andrea. Am I missing something here? You do love me, don't you?" he asked.

"Of course I do!" she groaned. "How could I not love you?"

"And you know I love you, don't you, Andi?" he stepped closer to her, but she backed away. He snapped the lid shut on the ring and sat down. "You are not going to say what I think you're going to say, are you?" he asked.

Andrea averted her gaze and Blake rolled his eyes.

"That is what you're thinking, isn't it?" He cracked his knuckles and threw his head back to stare at the ceiling. Andrea knew he was thinking. This was his thinking stance. In spite of herself, she giggled. His thinking stance was not one to be sculptured into marble and preserved for generations to come. He looked at her with the teasing glint that still made her heart do somersaults. He patted a place on the sofa beside him. She acquiesced and sat down next to him.

"We've been all through this, Andi. Dozens of times. Millions of times! What is this obsession you have with the difference in our ages? That is what's bothering you, isn't it?"

"Oh, Blake, it isn't an obsession. It's a fact. We may as well be light years apart in distance as to be this far apart in our ages," she said.

"Don't be ridiculous! Ten measly years! To hear you say it, you'd think you were on Medicare and I was in diapers! I don't care about our ages, Andi. What do I have to do to convince you of that?" He ran his hands through his thick, wavy hair. "It's a nonissue," he went on. "Why does it gnaw at you like this?"

"I don't know, Blake. It just does. What will we do in a few years when I need a nap and you need to take a run?"

"I suppose you'll nap and I'll run," he answered.

"What if you decide you want children?"

"We can have children. Children are from the Lord. If we're to have them, have them we will. I don't plan on losing any sleep over it."

"And there are so many women at work who. . ."

". . .are my age. Or younger. Who are available, who are glamorous, and who can outrun me. So what? I don't love any of them! In fact, I don't even like most of them!" He gave her a look of pained exasperation. "Andrea, I love you. I'll love you as long as I live. The only way for me to prove it to you is for you to say 'yes' and for us to get on with our lives together. The proof will be in the perseverance. I won't care if you end up in a wheelchair and I'm still running marathons. I won't care if I end up in a wheelchair and you run marathons! You can trust my love, Andrea. It's for keeps."

He embraced her and kissed her gently.

"Now," he said, reaching for the ring again. "No more kisses until this is on your finger. And this subject of age is closed. For good. The first time it comes to your mind again, you let me know and we'll go through all this again until you're convinced, okay?"

She let him slip the beautiful solitaire on her ring finger. "All right. And I accept your proposal of marriage, Blake Louis

Sanderson."

From that moment on and through their ten years of marriage and the arrival of their two children, she had not doubted his love again. Or feared losing him to another woman. Until now.

He had come home late from work. She had quit her job of twenty years once the boys were born and contentedly stayed home to homeschool their sons—and learn how to tackle the enormous task of a full-time wife and mother of twins. This week the boys were at church camp and she thought she and Blake would have hours to themselves—maybe take a quick day trip to the beach or King's Island. But on this first day of their week alone, Blake was surly and distracted. At first Andrea had thought it was just a work-related issue and tried to talk him out of his uncharacteristic dark mood.

"Bad day at work today, Blake?" she asked, handing him a glass of water while he proceeded to remove his tie and kick off his shoes.

"No. It was okay. It looks like the most recent restructuring isn't going to affect our department. I'm glad. I wasn't looking forward to giving anyone his or her walking papers." He took the water and continued to change clothes.

"Want to do anything special tonight? The boys are gone and—"

"I'm pretty tired, Andrea. Think I'll just take a run and come back and crash on the couch." He reached for his running shorts and pulled a pair of white socks from his drawer. "Maybe tomorrow, okay?" He finished the glass of water, tied his shoes, and rose to leave.

"Is something bothering. . . ?" she started to ask, but he abruptly left the room.

"I won't be long. Just a quick 10 K," he said and left.

Andrea sat on their bed. This was the first time in ten years he hadn't laughingly asked her to go running with him. It was part of their evening ritual. It was one of their private jokes. She had dismissed it, thinking she was being overly sensitive. When Blake returned from his run, however, his mood had not changed. For the first time in their lives, Andrea felt she had been shut out. They had talked, but she did most of the talking and the conversation was about nothing in particular. He had finally turned on the television set, also unusual for him, and sat in front of it for the rest of the evening, saying little and flipping through the newspaper and a runner's magazine. As they got into bed for the night, Andrea decided she had better try to find out once more what was troubling him.

"What is it, Blake? You haven't been yourself tonight," she said, propping herself up on an elbow and running her fingers across his forehead.

"Nothing, Andrea. Well," he said with a sigh, "not 'nothing,' but I don't want to talk about it. At least not tonight. Sorry to be so grouchy. We'll talk tomorrow, okay? I've got a few things to sort out in my head."

He turned away from her touch without a good night kiss. Andrea stared into the darkness and couldn't remember when she'd felt so alone.

When she had awakened, Blake had already left. He had taken a few days off work and they had planned to do some fun things together—just the two of them. Now she sat on the swing, anxiously waiting his return, hoping he would come home his usual invigorated, whistling self after his long run. She looked down at her hands. She was getting older. After birthing twin boys at forty, she had never quite gotten back the slender figure that had kept her looking young. Keeping her hair the same glossy brown it had been when she and Blake met dictated frequent trips to the salon. The varicose veins on her legs were not only unsightly, but would probably mandate some surgery in the not-too-distant future. She sighed. If anything, Blake was more physically attractive than ever. The graying at his temples softened the laugh lines around his eyes and he was as lean and muscular as when they first dated. She had been in the throes of midlife since the boys had traded their teething rings for bicycles and skateboards. Blake was just beginning midlife.

She tried to shake the foreboding, but couldn't. They had so many friends—even so-called Christian friends—whose marriages deteriorated when this dreaded decade of change hit. At least two couples she could think of had divorced. Both for the same reason: The man had found someone younger, more desirable.

"Stop it, Andrea!" she said aloud. "You're being ridiculous!" She shook her head to shake the wild imaginations away. The one time in their marriage her husband comes home from work with something less than a smile on his face, she goes to pieces! She was getting menopausal! Her changing hormones were wreaking havoc on her common sense! She got up from the swing and looked up the street. She saw Blake come around the corner, hands on his hips, his chest heaving from just completing his long morning run. She ran into the house, grabbed a bottle of sports drink from the refrigerator, and went to meet him.

"Good run?" she asked, holding out the container to him. He wiped his face with the bottom of his shirt and took the offered bottle from her.

"Thanks, Andi. Yeah, but it's humid. I'm glad I was able to run this morning." He took a long drink as they walked back to the house.

"Are you feeling better today? You weren't yourself last night, you know," she said gently, hoping to elicit more response than she had gotten last evening.

"Yeah, well, I've got a lot on my mind. What do you have planned for today?" he asked offhandedly.

"I thought we might go to King's Island or swimming. I could pack a picnic lunch for the two of us. . . ."

"I think I'm going to go into work for a few hours, Andi. Maybe we can do something after that." He finished the beverage as they walked around to the backyard. "I'm going to take a dip before I shower. Get me a towel, would you?" He sat down to remove his shoes and didn't look up.

"Sure," Andrea replied, taking the empty bottle and going to get him a towel.

She returned just in time to see him getting out of their pool. She tried once more. "Is something wrong, Blake? Anything you want to talk about?"

"Not now, Andrea. Thanks for the drink," he said, giving her a quick peck on the cheek and heading towards the house.

Blake's "few hours" turned into the rest of the day. When he got home after six o'clock, he was apologetic and conciliatory. Andrea was tense, angry, and not feeling very forgiving.

"We were supposed to have some time together this week, Blake. This is our one chance while Ben and Brandon are at camp." She was careful not to whine, but she only barely managed it. "You didn't even have the courtesy to call!"

"I know, Andi. I'm sorry. The day just got away from me. You could have called me," he said.

"I did. Henry said you were out for a long lunch."

"Oh. He didn't tell me you called. Sorry. I would have called you back. I should have called you. I've got a lot on my mind."

"Obviously," she said curtly and turned to go to the kitchen.

Blake followed her. "I'm sorry, Andi. Really. You know this isn't like me. We'll do something this week, I promise. I've got a board meeting at church tonight. Why don't we run and get a quick bite to eat somewhere?"

Their meal was a quick affair. Andrea noticed Blake ate little and she herself picked at her food. They talked about everything and nothing. She was still angry; he was still distracted. When he dropped her off at home, he made some last-minute comments.

"Don't wait up, Andrea. I think this will be a long one tonight. I'll see you in the morning or call from work tomorrow." With that, he drove away.

"Don't put yourself out," she muttered as the taillights rounded the corner. She spent the evening trying to read a book, but ended up crying and praying. She heard Blake come in after midnight. She muffled a sob and pretended to be asleep.

When Blake got up for work the next morning, Andrea feigned sleep again until after he left. She pored over Psalm 40, trying to gain back her equilibrium. After praying and studying the Bible passage for two hours, Andrea felt some measure of peace. She knew she was in a spiritual battle and she knew her fears and suspicions were not from the God who instructed her to trust Him. She decided to call Blake and simply weather his inexplicable moodiness until he was ready to tell her what was troubling him.

"Hi!" she said cheerily. "Want to meet for lunch at that little place around the corner from you?"

"I can't, Andrea. But I should be able to leave by two. Why don't you get some stuff together and we'll go to the beach when I get home? We'll have some dogs on the grill while we're there—just keep it simple." His voice sounded tired.

"All right, Blake. I'll have everything ready to go when you get home. See you then." They hung up and Andrea set about putting together a simple, but lavish picnic supper. She decided to go to a favorite deli of theirs and get some kosher wieners and a quart of the best cole slaw in the city. She felt more light-hearted than she had all week.

While she waited in line at the deli, she glanced around the attached restaurant. It certainly had become a busy place since she had first discovered it a year or so ago. Word of good food got around quickly! She was just about to turn back to the woman behind the counter when she saw Blake in a far booth, his back towards her. Her heart went to her throat. He was not alone. He was with a woman, a young, beautiful woman whom Andrea did not recognize. She was crying and Andrea saw Blake reach across the table to touch her face and wipe away a tear.

"Could I help you?" the woman behind the counter said loudly.

"I. . .no, no thank you. . ." Andrea managed to say and exited the deli. Tears immediately came to her eyes and she walked to her car almost blinded. She didn't know how long she sat in her car, shaking, weeping, and disbelieving.

This couldn't be happening! Not to her and Blake! She ached so inside she didn't think she would be able to keep breathing. She saw Blake come out of the delicatessen with the raven-haired beauty. He said a few words to her and embraced her before they walked separate ways to their parked cars. Andrea's weeping became sobs as she started her car and left another way up the street. She didn't know where to go. She had to go somewhere to think. . .to pour out her pain to God. Suddenly God did not seem as close as He had just an hour ago. She went home, put away what she had started to pack for their "day" together, and scrawled a hasty note to Blake.

"Had to check on mother. Will call and update you" was all she wrote. She packed a few things in a small suitcase and left the house. She hadn't said her mother was any worse. He would think she had had another ministroke and that the nursing home had called to inform Andrea. She hadn't lied to him. That was more than he had done for her! Work indeed! She slammed the door and jumped in the car. She headed north towards the extended care facility to visit her mother.

"Hi, Mrs. Sanderson!" said the nurse as Andrea walked towards her mother's room. "Didn't expect to see you again so soon. There's no change. Your mom is out on the porch for some fresh air."

"Thank you," Andrea replied, walking back outside. Her mother was alone, tied in a wheelchair, her chin on her chest. Andrea's tears had dried. She felt exhausted and sank into a chair near her elderly mother. She touched her frail hand and Cora looked up, her expression blank.

"Hi, Mama. It's me, Andrea." Andrea leaned over to kiss her mother's cheek. Her mother's hair smelled like baby shampoo. It had been pulled up into a small bun and a pink ribbon was pinned in place above it. Andrea had never had regrets about choosing this nursing care facility. Her mother got wonderful care—down to the littlest details.

"I just wanted to check on you today, Mama. I'm glad to see you're out in this warm sunshine. It's a nice change from your room, isn't it?"

Cora continued to stare at Andrea in silence. Andrea always talked to her as if she could hear and understand her. She never assumed just because her mother did not speak or show recognition that she was not conscious of her surroundings or visitors. Andrea liked to think that her mother understood everything going around about her, that she simply wasn't able to show it in any way.

"I had to come and see you, Mama. I'm afraid. . ." Andrea choked back a sob, glad for the solitude she and her mother had outside here. "I'm afraid I'm losing Blake. . .that I've already lost him." She paused to dry her tears with a shaking hand. "I don't know what to do, Mama. You know I was always afraid of something like this. Blake is so young and handsome. . .I knew it was only a matter of time before some other—oh, Mama, what am I going to do?" Andrea wept brokenly, quietly, holding onto her mother's hand.

That night Andrea stayed in a hotel close to the nursing home. She had talked and read to her mother through the day, and pushed her around the grounds in the wheelchair. When she went to the hotel, Andrea wept and cried out to God. She could neither eat nor sleep. She called when she was sure Blake would be at church. She left a message telling him everything was fine, that she was spending some time with her mother for another day.

On Thursday evening she came to say good-bye to her mother and then drive home—to what, she didn't know. She had no plan. Should she confront Blake? Should she try to get him to tell her what he was doing? What about the boys? What would she tell them? She was too overwhelmed to be able to sort out any of it.

She entered her mother's room. Blake looked up, his face etched with worry. Andrea stopped, surprised to find him there.

"Andi. Where have you been?" he asked, coming to her. "I was worried sick!"

Andrea shrank from his touch and prayed not to make a fool of herself. She skirted around to the other side of Cora's bed and gave her mother a kiss.

"Bye, Mama. I'll be back next week," she said. Blake looked at Andrea questioningly, but turned back to Cora and gave her a kiss too.

"See you, Mama Wicks. We'll bring the boys next time."

He took Andrea's arm as she came around the bed to the door and he walked outside with her, neither of them speaking. Andrea's stomach was in knots. She didn't know if she should run, stand there and scream at Blake, or walk away without a word.

"I'll follow you home, Andi. We need to talk," he said quietly.

"About you or me or Mother?" she asked.

"Your mom seems unchanged to me. Is that right?" he asked as they continued walking.

"Yes," she answered, not sure her legs would carry her all the way to her car.

"Then I guess it's about you and me," he said.

"And. . . ?" she prompted.

"And. . . ?" he asked, his expression puzzled.

She didn't answer. Her tears were too close to spilling over. She got into her car and drove home, never once looking into the rearview mirror.

When they got home, the telephone was ringing. Blake answered it and Andrea could tell it was the boys.

"Well, we're glad you're having such a good time, Ben. You're both staying out of trouble?" A pause. "In that case, you'd better let me talk to your brother." Blake covered the receiver. "Pick up the other phone, Andi. It's the boys," he said. He spoke into the telephone again as Andi climbed the stairs to their bedroom. She heard the last of Blake's reprimand to the oldest twin.

"Got anything to say to your mom?" Blake asked.

"Hi, honey," Andrea said. "We miss you guys!"

"This is the neatest place, Mom! I wish we could stay another week!" Brandon answered.

"We're glad you guys called back," Blake said. "We'll pick you up at church on Saturday. And no more throwing food in the cafeteria, Brandon. Is that understood?"

"Yes, Pop. See you Saturday! Ben wants to say 'hi' to Mom. . . ."

"Hi, Mom. You and Pop having fun without us?"

Andrea hoped her voice didn't quaver. "We're trying, Ben. It's not easy without you two! Is your asthma acting up?" she asked, changing the subject.

"Nah. I haven't had to use my inhaler once. Well, we gotta go. Some other kids want to make some calls. See you, Mom. See ya, Pop!" A few more good-byes and they hung up. Andrea sat on the bed, willing her tears not to start. She went to the bathroom, took a shower, and did her best to wash away any traces of her hours of tears and lack of sleep. Blake was waiting for her when she came out. He had changed into shorts and a tee shirt.

"Let's go out to the pool," he said. Although he said it gently, it was more of an order than a suggestion. He draped an arm around Andrea's shoulders as they descended the stairs together. When they got outside, Andrea noticed he had some lemonade and a bag of pretzels sitting on the patio table.

"Okay, my dear wife. I'm sorry I spoiled our week by going into work so much. I promise not to even check my voice mail tomorrow. Would you tell me why you stayed overnight in a hotel less than two hours from your house?"

"I. . .just didn't feel like driving home again yesterday," she replied. "Besides, you've been so distracted that I figured I wouldn't be missed."

"I am so sorry, Andi. I know I haven't been much of a communicator lately. I've had. . ."

". . .a lot on your mind," she finished for him. "I know,"

she said, looking at him. "When you weren't saying it with words, you were saying it without them." She bit her lower lip to stop it from quivering.

"Andi," he said and pulled her to him, kissing her hair and neck. She closed her eyes to hide her tears and to harden herself against his touch. He led her to the love seat and kissed her eyelids and mouth.

"I am so sorry," he whispered. "I've handled this so badly where you're concerned. I haven't wanted to keep this from you, but I didn't know how to tell you. I was late coming home after the board meeting the other night because I asked the pastor to go have a cup of coffee with me so I could talk to him. I should have talked to you first. He even told me that."

I don't want to hear this, Andrea said to herself. She was trembling and her stomach was hurting again. She wanted to pull away from Blake, but she wanted to will him back to her by keeping close to him. *Dear Jesus*, she prayed, *let him ask me for forgiveness and not for a divorce. Please. Please.*

"I don't know where to start," Blake said, leaning back and holding her hand tightly.

"How about at the beginning?" she suggested.

"That's like going too far back," he said, throwing his head back and rubbing his eyes with his free hand.

Oh, God, Andrea cried inside. *How long has this been going on? Is she the first?*

"I've. . .I don't know how to say this, but just to say it, Andi. I've got a daughter. A twenty-two-year-old daughter."

Andrea's head came up with a start. She didn't have time to say anything as the words tumbled from Blake in rapid succession.

"On Monday this beautiful young woman came into my office and said—with no preamble—'Hello, Daddy.' I thought maybe she was talking to Bert, but he wasn't at his desk. 'Excuse me?' I replied. 'Can I help you?' She sat down in front of me and was quiet for the space of a full minute. Then she said, 'Do you remember Nancy Weber? I'm her daughter. I'm your daughter.' " Blake stood and paced before Andrea, who still sat in a numbing shock. He ran his hands through his hair.

"A daughter, Andrea. I've got a daughter I never knew I had until three days ago! She walked into my life—into our lives— and suddenly my world is upside down! I'm sorry I didn't tell you right away. I wasn't sure she was telling the truth, although my gut told me she was. On Tuesday I made some calls and verified her story. Yesterday I met her for lunch at Goldstein's and we had a long talk. There's so much I have to tell you and say to you, Andi. I don't know where to begin. She's an impetuous kid and somewhat given to theatrics. Her waltzing into my office and making a paternity announcement almost gave me a heart attack!" He continued to pace.

Andrea didn't know whether to laugh or cry. Her emotions had gone from despair to shock to shame and back to shock again in as many seconds as Blake had been talking. His agitation was in stark contrast to her calliope of feelings. He had not been untrue to her—how could she have ever suspected him of such a thing? The only one Blake loved more than her was the Lord Jesus Christ. He could not, would not, be untrue to her because he would never be untrue to his God. He was too much a man of God to do anything like that! He had never, ever given her any reason to doubt his love or devotion. Yet she had allowed unsubstantiated, poisonous suspicions to rob her of the opportunity to simply be there for her husband in a crisis neither of them could have ever imagined! She was ashamed of her lack of trust. . .in Blake and in the Lord. She whispered a prayer of repentance to God and went to wrap her arms around her husband.

"I'm sorry too, Blake. Sorry I wasn't here when you needed me. How can this be true?"

"You remember before we were married I told you I wasn't chaste as a young man. It only happened once, Andrea. I was still in high school at the time. I was so ashamed and afraid my parents would find out, and that my dad would lose his church or something, that I was determined never to do it again. And before I grew much older, I finally surrendered myself to Jesus. He helped me stay pure just as the fear was wearing off from that night with Nancy. But all of this you already knew." He stopped and cracked his knuckles. "What I didn't know was that this girl, Nancy Weber, got pregnant that night. Nancy was a virgin too. I've absolutely no doubt about that. We were two kids who pushed each other's buttons until things got out of hand. She moved away shortly afterward and I never heard from her. Her parents were wonderful people and stood by her. They never forced her to consider abortion and, for whatever reason, Nancy never sought to give Robyn—our daughter—up for adoption. Robyn has told me all this over the course of the last few days. Just before Nancy died of breast cancer last year, she finally told Robyn who her father was. Robyn started her search soon after Nancy's death and, well, here she is! Nancy's folks barely remember me, according to Robyn. She told them my name before coming here."

Blake stopped talking and sighed deeply. "I still can't believe this." He got up and walked away from Andrea. He sat down at the edge of the pool, swishing the water around with his legs. "Do you know, Nancy never even told her parents who Robyn's father was? She only told Robyn when it was clear she wasn't going to survive the cancer. She never married, so I'm Robyn's closest relative. What are we going to tell the boys?" he asked abruptly.

Andrea slipped off her sandals and sat next to Blake. She was pensive and had already let go of her own troubled thoughts. She and Blake had something more pressing and real to address now. Blake was a father to a daughter. She was a stepmother. Their boys had a stepsister more than twice their age. How would they take this news?

"Have you told Robyn about us? About our family?" she asked.

"Yeah. She saw the picture of the four of us on my desk at work and has asked a lot of questions about you and the boys. She's pretty disconnected right now, as you can well imagine. She begins crying every time the subject of her mother comes up, which is understandable. Nancy was a dentist and left Robyn well taken care of financially. She attends Indiana University and her schooling is all paid for out of a trust. She's not here for money, that's for sure. Her grandparents and an uncle and his family are a good support system for her. She lives with her grandparents when she's home from school during the summer. She's staying with a friend from IU while she's here in town."

"What's she like? I mean, what are your first impressions of her?" Andrea asked, glad to be able to have this long talk with her husband. He thought before answering.

"Dramatic. Expressive. Extroverted. She's a good conversationalist and a good listener. She seems to have high moral standards, but she has little church background. She seemed mildly interested when I talked to her of my own spiritual life and relationship with the Lord Jesus, but she skirted away from the topic as I got more personal with my questions on her own spirituality. She's a beautiful young lady, Andrea. She reminds me a lot of my mother's sister, Rita. She's got a lot of the Italian side of my family in her looks. She's quite charming, to tell you the truth. I think she'll be easy to learn to love. For all four of us." He picked up her hand and kissed it. "What consequences come of our actions! Even years later. . ." He continued to hold her hand and his gaze drifted over the water.

"Well, what's our first order of business? Does she seem to have any interest in moving here with us?" Andrea asked.

"No. She wants to stay in touch, maybe visit on some holidays. She wants to take this slowly. As dramatic as her 'Hello, Daddy' was, I don't think she's ready to come crashing into our lives anytime soon. She wants to meet you, but said she'd rather meet the boys later. She'd like us to 'test the waters,' as she put it, before making that step. In fact, she plans to leave by Saturday. I'm going to have some difficult days ahead, Andrea. I'm glad you're here with me. I never told my parents about the incident with Nancy. I never told anyone but you about that. How we're going to explain it to the boys, I have no idea." He hesitated and brought his eyes back to Andrea's. "Robyn is. . .because of me. I now have the same reminder of that night that Nancy lived with. The lives of a lot of people are never going to be the same."

"Robyn is here not only because of you, Blake. She is first of all God's. She is here because of God Himself. He brought her into being. He has a plan for her. It looks like His plan for her includes us now. Like our times with my mother and when your brother died, we'll simply take each day at a time and help Robyn as much as we can and as much as she allows us. You know I'll support you every inch of the way. I. . .trust you, Blake. I know you'll make the right decisions and do the right things. And we'll garner enough prayer support to see us through the hardest parts."

"Like going to Nancy's parents and asking their forgiveness," he said softly.

"Yes. 'Like going to Nancy's parents and asking their forgiveness,' " she repeated.

"I love you, Mrs. Sanderson. Do you know that?" he asked, looking at her with a small smile.

"Yes, I do, Mr. Sanderson. I'll never doubt it." They kissed briefly and Andrea relished the tender look in the eyes of her husband.

Someday she would confess her own sin to him: her lack of trust in his love. Today would not be the day, however. They were facing an abrupt change in their uncomplicated, wonderful life as a family. God had given them this wonderful life. God had given them each other. God had given them their two wonderful boys. And now God had given them Robyn. With God, with their trust in Him and each other, they would see the good that would come of it all. . .together.

CHAPTER 2

Contentment

Each heart knows its own bitterness. . .
—Proverbs 14:10 NIV

Amy glanced at her watch for the third time in as many minutes. If there was anything she hated more than this incessant waiting, she didn't know what it was. She was convinced every physician's office in her territory subscribed to the same three or four magazines. As she mindlessly turned the pages in last month's edition of *Family Days,* she was sure she had seen this copy—complete with some coupons ripped out—in every waiting room she had sat in for the last six weeks. And she had sat in a lot of them.

If she had known when she went into medical sales that she would spend endless hours in her car, frustratingly long, additional hours stuck in traffic, and still more time sitting in physicians' waiting rooms hoping to make one lousy sale, she would have opted for a far more exciting profession. Even working in the auto parts factory a number of summers while in college was better than this. What she wouldn't give now to be making that kind of money and keeping busy! So what if the work was boring and the factory was usually 85 degrees? It was better than this sitting and waiting!

She looked around the room discreetly. It had been packed with people ten minutes ago. Now she and a young mother with three small children were the only ones left. The mother held the newborn she had just finished nursing and reached to restrain a toddler who was attempting to climb onto one of the many small tables around the room. Another child was lying on the carpet, absorbed in trying to change the clothes on her baby doll. All of them were dressed in what Amy was sure were designer clothes—probably even the baby, though she couldn't tell around the blanket.

It must be nice, she thought. *Coming in from the 'burbs after Nanny got the kids all dolled up for a visit to the doctor's office.* The Perfect Little Mother sat there without a hair out of place, her clothes immaculate, and her delicate, manicured fingernails outdone only by the diamond tennis bracelet that glittered on one dainty wrist. *How does a woman with three small children—one of them a newborn—manage to be so slender?* Amy wondered.

She went back to her magazine, but her interest waned even before she read two sentences. She glanced again at the baby. How long would it be before she and Christopher would have children? The wedding was nine months away. His doctorate degree was at least that far away and then some. She didn't see how they could hope to start their family for another few years. She sighed and held back the tears that threatened every time she started to think of the future. The future without her mother, who had always been her best friend.

In some ways she still could not believe it. The diagnosis said her mother would not live another year. Her mother! She was only fifty-eight years old! How could this be? Yet, when she rushed home after receiving her father's telephone call, she knew the truth. One look at her previously robust, healthy mom said it all. It had only been six weeks since she had last seen her and she could hardly believe the change. Her mother had lost so much weight and her skin had a sickly yellow hue to it. Amy had planned to go in with a chipper, upbeat "we'll beat this!" attitude, but her plans dissolved to tears when she entered her mother's hospital room. She had wept, just as her father had wept when he called her to come home. She and her brothers and sister sat with their parents while the doctor used words like "comfortable" and "palliative" as he outlined what could be expected in the course of the following weeks.

"Recovery" and "cure" were not words he used.

What will I do without you, Mom? she asked herself. Her mom would not be there on her wedding day. She would not be there to spoil the grandchildren she and Chris would have brought to her. She would not be there. Period. Her closest confidante, friend, and encourager. . . . Amy couldn't imagine her life without her mother. She didn't want to imagine life without her mother! But it was there, and it was inescapable. *Why, God? Why my mother?*

"Molly, sweetheart, don't pull your ribbons loose! Grandma is waiting for you to come over and show them to her!" The young mother spoke quietly to her oldest child, interrupting Amy's thoughts.

Amy looked back to the magazine on her lap. There would be no trips to Grandma's to show off ribbons for any daughters she would ever have! Christopher's mother had died years ago; her mother's death would come shortly. It must be nice to have no problems beyond worrying about your daughter pulling the ribbons from her hair before going to Grandma's! Amy looked at her watch again and muted her weary sigh.

Tough life, Perfect Little Mother. At least your children have a "Grandma's" to go to. She bit back her threatening tears and turned what attention she could muster back to the dog-eared magazine.

Noelle gently placed her newborn son back into the stroller. She was glad this would be Max's last well-baby visit to the doctor's for a while. She reached again for her active toddler, attempting to entice him to play with a bucket of blocks she had placed in the back of Max's stroller. Micah seemed content for the moment to begin stacking them, following his mother's lead. Noelle was able to reach over and quickly adjust one of Molly's dangling ribbons.

"Why don't you sit at the table, Molly? That carpet is probably not very clean," she said. Molly's concentration on her dolls did not wane. Neither did she move from the floor. Noelle sighed quietly, not willing to battle over something so unimportant. She could imagine what Cliff would have said had he heard her.

"That's the trouble with you, Noelle. You're forever giving the kids a choice! You're the adult! TELL them what to do! Don't ask!"

Well, Cliff hadn't heard her. He wouldn't be hearing anything else from her either. She had come home from a long weekend at her parents' home to a house emptied of Cliff's clothes, Cliff's books, Cliff's condescending tone, and Cliff himself.

"I'm sorry, Noelle," his note had said. "There's someone else and I can't keep up this charade anymore. My lawyer will call you to settle everything. You and the kids will be well taken care of."

He had called her that night, tightly apologetic, but telling her in his usual, brusque manner that she would not have any financial worries. He would want to have the kids "at least once a month," but that he was going out of town on business soon, so maybe not *this* month. "You'll manage," he had said smoothly. "You always have before." He had begun to assure her again that he knew his "responsibility," as he called it, to them and would continue to provide for the children, but she had hung up quietly while he was still talking. The next time she had heard from Cliff was through his lawyer, just as he had promised.

In one way she had not been surprised. He had been growing more distant since before Max was born. She had tried to talk to him, tried to learn what was troubling him, but he retreated even further. She was not a bold person; her timidity was in direct contrast to Cliff's "take the bull by the horns" assertiveness. He had once told her that was the first thing that attracted him to her: her shy, quiet demeanor. She was so unlike him that he thought they would make the perfect match. She thought that too. . .once.

Life had had a way of turning their contrasts into conflicts—their differences into sharp disagreements. She wanted him home more; he wanted to be out with friends and clients. She wanted to go to church together as a family; he needed Sundays to sleep in or golf with a client. She wanted to have family or another couple over for a nice evening of small talk and familiarity; he wanted big, catered parties to impress people she didn't know and to whom he seldom introduced her. She wanted children; he had grudgingly consented to one. When she became pregnant with Micah, Cliff only stopped belittling her for her "carelessness" when he found out they were going to have a son. Noelle had not had her tubes tied after Micah's birth; she had had a terrible time with postpartum depression. By the time she felt ready to schedule the surgery, she was pregnant again. Cliff had been beside himself with anger.

"I can't believe you did this again!" he had almost shouted, something he never did. "What in the world are we going to do with three kids? You can barely manage the two we've got!"

She had bit back words like "I didn't do this alone, you know" and had silently taken his wrath. He had apologized—as much as his pride allowed him—later, but she thought now that it was then his long hours and days away from home grew longer and closer together. He was driven by the need to control and to make money. His work provided him with both in generous measure. In her own quiet way, Noelle had been forced to be mom, dad, and household manager. She did it because it had to be done. She saw it as a necessity; Cliff saw it as her encroachment on his "turf." But, as it turned out, it wasn't turf he was interested in fighting for. *After all, it was only his home and kids,* she mused. He had "bigger fish to fry," as he was fond of telling her, out in the "real world."

Somewhere in his world of money and power plays he had met a woman like himself, she suspected. Although he had always provided for her and the kids to the point of extravagance, she thought now it was more out of pride than love. It was just one more way to show everyone he had "made it" in the "real world." So she, Noelle, was left with the big house (and big utility bills), a new minivan (with a large monthly payment), expensive health insurance for herself, a pittance for alimony (in spite of Cliff's earlier reassurances to the contrary), and less child support than she had hoped for. The ache in her heart that threatened to overwhelm her at least-expected moments was one more thing she hadn't anticipated. Cliff was not a perfect husband and father, but they had had many happy moments. She remembered them. He, apparently, did not.

Micah's smile was so much his father's. It would bring to mind the times Cliff would smile at her that way. Molly had picked up her father's propensity for water sports. Cliff had been around so little after Max's birth that he alone of their three children did not cause her to have flashbacks of happier times. She wasn't sure she could do this alone. Granted, she had been doing a lot that should have fallen to Cliff. But when things did get to be too much, he had been there if she needed him.

Cliff had taken care of so many things, in spite of his long absences and frequent long days at the office. Noelle had ended up in tears the last two times she had tried to balance the checkbook. And now the central air-conditioning was acting up. She had no idea whom to call! And she wasn't sure what to do about the TDA Cliff had set up for her when they first married. Or did she not do anything? Should she sell the stocks that she had? Should she buy a smaller house? There were so many—too many —decisions to be made! She was sure it was only the children who kept her from completely falling apart. She had to be there, and be strong, for them. But it was so hard. . . .

She looked over at the other woman who sat in the waiting room. Noelle noticed the simple engagement ring on her finger and the briefcase on the floor next to her. *What a simple life she must have!* she thought. *Probably gets to fly all over the country and meets exciting people all the time. Her whole life is ahead of her! I'll bet,* Noelle thought to herself, *she doesn't have a care in the world. If this doctor doesn't want to buy whatever she's selling, the next one will. She'll just jet off to her next destination and pick up her paycheck between exotic stops. It would be nice to be that carefree, if only for a day. . . . Dear Jesus,* she prayed, *help me through this. How I wish I could have a life as simple as hers!*

"Mrs. Harris?" a nurse opened the door to admit Noelle to the doctor's office. Noelle gathered up the toys and children as quickly as she could, directing Molly to push Max's stroller while she hoisted Micah to her hip. She passed Amy who continued to sit and wait. She gave her a weak smile of encouragement as if to say: *"Hold on. You're up next!"* Amy gave her a wan smile in return.

Both women were surprised to see a hint of tears in the other's eyes.

CHAPTER 3

The Passing

*"See that you do not look down on one of these little ones.
For I tell you that their angels in heaven always
see the face of my Father in heaven."*
—Matthew 18:10 NIV

How could something that had begun with such pure joy and excitement come to this?

Like an obedient child, Maureen donned the surgical mask and cover gown that the nurse quietly handed her. The doctor who had come to talk with her stood by silently, and Maureen thought how surreal this room was now. It had been busy with people and activity only minutes ago. Now the silence was a smothering, oppressive weight that stifled her breathing, slowed her movements, and paralyzed her speech. She followed the man out the door, but felt no relief in her escape from the room that had enclosed her like a shroud. She felt as though she were going to her death. She *was* going to a death. But it was not hers.

A collage of recent events came unbidden to her mind as she

came closer to the door which read: *NO ADMITTANCE. SUR-GICAL AREA.* She remembered the day eight months earlier when her daughter had called, her voice shrill with excitement.

"You're going to be a grandma again, Mom!" she announced. "Maybe this time you'll get a little girl to dress up in bows and ribbons."

Maureen was as happy as Alexis. This would be her third grandchild; maybe it *would* be a girl this time! She and Lexi, the boys, and their dad had celebrated the good news with a dinner out that evening. The pregnancy had begun so marvelously! Alexis was never sick a day. The inevitable tiredness was a motivational catalyst that spurred the boys to activities like helping with the laundry and making their beds without any reminder. But Lexi's first sonogram had tolled a menacing bell. The excitement had disappeared. A pall replaced the happy anticipation.

Obvious defects marred the developing child who was the hoped-for little girl. One leg and one arm were malformed. A stomach could not be seen and other major organs did not look to be in the right positions. The obstetrician suggested abortion. Alexis changed doctors, but that did not change the diagnosis or the worsening pictures that came with each ultrasound. Her new obstetrician was sympathetic and supportive, but he offered no encouragement other than "the best that can be done for the baby will be done." His next statement had haunted Maureen's thoughts for the subsequent months, despite her attempts to forget it and trust God for a miracle.

"But in the end," he had said, "I'm afraid it will make little difference in the ultimate outcome."

Ultimate outcome. Such a clean, antiseptic, impersonal way to say: "I'm sorry, but your baby will not live to smile her first smile, play with her older brothers, or have her daddy walk her down the aisle." Maureen had agonized through the stages of sorrow, anger, and denial with Alexis, Drew, and the boys in the ensuing months. Like waves of the Pacific, each emotion had battered them into a kind of worn submission, waiting for Chelsea's arrival with pained anticipation. *Perhaps,* they said to themselves and each other, *it won't be as bad as they say. Maybe we will be blessed with a miracle we can shower with love for years to come—with or without handicaps.*

Maureen had watched her daughter and son-in-law bravely answer the questions of well-meaning friends. She had also watched as a wall of isolation grew slowly up and around her previously social daughter and family. Some friends stood by them, but many found their presence disquieting—a painful reminder that life wasn't always full of hopeful expectation. . .that sometimes the future was a specter that reached relentlessly for you, pushing hope and optimism aside with powerful tentacles. And in fear for themselves, some friends kept a safe distance away. Maureen had not been allowed such a net of safety. Even now, Alexis slept. For Maureen there was no anesthesia to hold the specter at bay for a few more minutes. She walked through the electronic door beside the physician like a woman in a dream, but her mind was reeling with events of the day.

Lexi's labor had come early. The boys were at their cousins' farm one hundred miles away. Drew wasn't one hundred miles away; he was thousands of miles away. A business trip and dense fog kept him trapped in an airport hours from his wife and newborn daughter. And the trip and fog had kept him from her, his mother-in-law, who now had a burden thrust upon her that she could not escape. The touch of the physician's hand upon her elbow brought her from her thoughts to what she must now do and say. He spoke first.

"We've been working with the baby for over twenty minutes

now. She did have a heartbeat when she was born, but she has not moved or taken a breath. We've been doing the breathing for her, have given her medication to try and increase her heart rate, but she has shown no response. But we need your permission to discontinue our efforts." His voice was gentle, quiet, and his words chosen carefully, she thought. She could only nod her head in mute submission and followed him into the bright room where two other people hovered over her only grand-daughter. One rhythmically pressed her fingers onto the baby's chest and the other masked-and-gloved woman just as rhythmically stood squeezing a bag that was attached to a tube that came from her granddaughter's mouth. She could only see their eyes; eyes that in her brief glance at them confirmed the words the doctor continued to speak in measured tones.

She looked at Chelsea's bruised head. Her body was covered with dried blood from the birth. She did not move except for the up and down, up and down of her tiny chest with the breath forced into it. Maureen could not stop a sudden sob that came from her heart to her mouth. She reached to touch Chelsea's hand, to put her finger in the loosely clasped fingers that did not respond to her touch. Chelsea's still form blurred as tears filled Maureen's eyes. The pain from deep within threatened to swallow her, suffocate her. The specter no longer reached for her; it held her viselike, making her breathing a gulping for air.

The doctor continued to talk, to explain what had been done, what was being done. The cadence of his voice matched the pumping action of the gloved fingers on her only grand-daughter's chest. Maureen nodded her head in mute reply, but her concentration was on the face of Chelsea. Her matted hair was dark like Drew's and she noticed the downward slant of her fine eyebrows, so like Andy's. Except for the dried blood and bruising, Chelsea's face was perfect—dark eyelashes that rested on her cheeks and a tiny chin that reminded Maureen of Alexis when she was born.

"We need to ask your permission to stop our efforts here, Mrs. Lewis. There's really nothing more we can do," the doctor said, his death words spoken kindly. She couldn't say the word, but simply nodded her head. The pumping stopped; the bag squeezing ceased. The nurse put a stethoscope to Chelsea's chest and a finger and thumb on the umbilical cord stump from which protruded a length of clear tubing.

"I don't hear anything," she said. "But I can still feel a faint, slow beat." A beep on a monitor somewhere close confirmed what she said.

Maureen continued to hold her granddaughter's tiny, limp hand. Her grief threatened to swallow her whole. Her throat felt constricted, her stomach a knot. She wanted to pray, but she couldn't even begin. She felt a part of her own life was ebbing away as surely as Chelsea's was.

"My. . .daughter. Alexis. Is she awake? Is she all right?" she managed to say.

The physician removed his mask. For some reason, seeing his entire face brought a measure of calm to Maureen's aching heart and tangled emotions. She wished she could remove her mask too; it only made her breathing all the harder. The doctor seemed to read her thoughts.

"You can remove your mask," he said, which she did. The woman who had been breathing for Chelsea handed her some much-needed tissues. The doctor continued to speak. "Your daughter is fine. She'll be taken back to her room in just a few minutes. She's going to be drowsy for a while, but you can go see her anytime you want."

Maureen was torn between staying with Chelsea and going to Alexis. There were two in her family who needed her now, but she was only one person. Chelsea's heart still beat out slowly, but rhythmically on the monitor. She gasped infrequently. Should she stay here or go be with her daughter? How she wished Drew were here!

"Would you like to hold her?" the nurse asked.

Maureen looked at her in surprise. "Oh, could I?" she asked. To hold Chelsea while she still had life! She could die in the loving embrace of her grandmother and not on some open, hard, sterile hospital bed!

"Of course!"

Within seconds a rocking chair was pushed into the cramped room and Maureen gratefully sat in it while the nurse tenderly bundled her granddaughter. She gave Chelsea to Maureen whose tears streamed down afresh as she held her granddaughter to her breast and immediately began rocking her.

"If you're comfortable, we'll leave you alone with Chelsea. I'll get a camera so we can take some pictures of her."

Alone in the room, Maureen began to sing softly an old Irish lullaby she had sung to all her children when they were born. In the midst of her own pain, she drew comfort from the still form she cradled in her arms as she sang the simple, old tune. With a curious mingling of heartache, the unanswered "why?" and hope, Maureen sang her song.

"Too-ra-loo-ra-loo-ral, too-ra-loo-ra-li, too-ra-loo-ra-loo-ral, Hush now, don't you cry. . ."

She brushed the fine eyebrows of her grandchild with the tip of her finger. Although her heart was aching and her tears continued to fall, Maureen knew that ultimately, finally, this would not be the end of her story with Chelsea. Of her life with Chelsea. But this parting was, like others she had endured, so very painful. She grieved because she would never play games with Chelsea. She would never hold her tight during a thunderstorm.

She would never witness her blush at the mention of her first boyfriend's name. Simply thinking on all this made her heart ache all the more. . .

But as she hummed her timeworn melody and wiped the teardrops that fell from her eyes onto the still face of her only granddaughter, Maureen allowed her thoughts to drift to a day yet future. A day when, as one of her favorite passages in the Bible said it, there would be "no more death or mourning or crying or pain for the old order of things" would be past. A tearless day. A day without grief. A day without the loss of a hoped-for little girl.

Chelsea's eyes would not be closed; they would be open and sparkling with pure joy and life. Her hair would not be matted with blood, but curled about her face like burnished gold. Her hands would not be limp and white, but held out in eager reception for her. Her voice would not be silent, but ringing with immeasurable joy:

"You sang me into the arms of Jesus, Grandmother! Welcome home!"

CHAPTER 4

Letting Go

A word aptly spoken is like apples of gold in settings of silver.
—Proverbs 25:11 NIV

Why can't this man just plain shut up for the space of five minutes and give me time to think?

I was secretly watching my daughter weave her web of temptation around the young man who had come to see her. Arthur had come in the back door and glanced briefly at Belle and Ian before he had settled in and taken to his philosophizing out loud, which he often did. It was his most annoying habit. He sat down near me. His incessant prattle was like the constant droning of a fly. It was about to drive me over the edge. I hoped to communicate as much by simply turning away from him. It didn't work.

"Don't be puttin' on that attitude with me, Starr," he said again, as if there was something the matter with my hearing. "That daughter of yours is just like you: independent, hardheaded, set on doin' things her way. I know we both raised her better, but there's no changin' it. Besides, you better take a minute to look at your reflection in Mirror Lake. It's just history repeatin' itself. Yep," he said, shaking his head, "just like you and me when we first met."

Arthur whittled a bit more on the piece of wood he held. I watched my long-legged daughter saucily throw her head back, trying to entice the young man who was already obviously intrigued with her. Watching his reaction to her antics, I guessed she was getting the attention and response she wanted. He smiled and beckoned to her, but she teasingly backed away from him, lowering her rich brown eyes as if to say "no" to his gentle persuasion. Arthur interrupted my train of thought. Again.

"Yep, that young Ian has an eye for her. He knows a prize when he sees one."

I tried to ignore Arthur's babbling. He was speaking of my Belle like she was a side of meat or some squawking pig at a county fair. She was neither. She had beauty, grace, bearing, and a pedigree that stretched back for generations. More than could be said for Arthur—*that* was for sure.

"She's old enough to make her own choices, Starr. You may have taken a shine to that O'Leary kid, but it's this English lad that's turned her pretty head. I like him myself. He'll treat her like a lady—just like I do you."

Harumph. Like you know how to treat someone of my breeding, you old coot. I'd like to kick what few teeth you have left in that face of yours right into. . .

"Remember when we first met? I don't think your mama approved of me none, either," he droned on, once again interrupting my own musings. "But when it was all said and done, she let you go with her blessing. And you ain't regretted it a day since and you know it, Starr."

I knew he was looking at me with that silly, lopsided grin of his. And that he was peering at me through his even sillier glasses that rested halfway down his crooked nose. But I wasn't giving him the satisfaction of looking his way or answering him. *I'll give you something to regret if you don't shut up,* I thought. But I kept the thought to myself. I shifted more, hoping my intensity on Belle would silence his rambling monologue. If for just *once* he'd be quiet and stop jabbering. . . !

"Yep, she's a beauty, that Belle. Just like her mama. Good thing she didn't inherit your sour disposition, Starr."

I jerked my head around in astonishment. Since when did Arthur think my disposition was anything less than impeccable? Perhaps my thoughts were occasionally less than noble, but I had always conducted myself properly—just as I was taught!

"I thought that'd get your attention," he said, cackling like an old hen. "You've gotten pretty high-and-mighty here of late—puttin' on airs, actin' like you're the queen mother or somethin'. You know I love you as much as my own, late, dear wife. . . ."

May God rest her sweet soul, I mouthed quietly, knowing those to be his oft-repeated, predictable next words.

"May God rest her sweet soul," he intoned. I smirked to myself. "But you sure don't make it easy, lady. Ever since you birthed Belle—and it's been years now—you've needed an attitude adjustment."

Self-centered lout. I turned away from him again, seeing what new web Belle was weaving around her captivated young man. I was sure both of them were oblivious to my attention and Arthur's presence. She certainly was giving a performance! And that insipid Ian wasn't the only one who was watching it! She would get the talking-to of her life when this nonsense was over!

I heard the front legs of Arthur's chair hit the floor. I saw out of the corner of my eye that he was watching Belle with keen interest now too.

He came over to stand beside me, letting his knife and the

piece of wood he was working on hang at his side. "Look at her," he said quietly. "Reminds me of the day you took to showin' off for me."

Showing off for him? I had never and would never give this man the satisfaction of—

"You remember, Starr?" he asked, his voice taking on that velvet edge that could tame a hornet. I could feel my defenses and arguments begin melting with that gentle tone of voice. Steeling myself against it was futile. I knew it, and wouldn't I be taken for a donkey if he didn't know it too!

"We were both a lot younger then, weren't we, sweet lady?" His free hand caressed me and all my haughtiness started ebbing away.

"I'll never forget the day we met. It was out at the Cutler place. Remember? You stood out in the crowd even before you noticed me looking at you. Everything about you spoke elegance, grace. . . . Even before you starting showing off for me— don't you deny it now—I knew you and me was in for the long haul. And here we are today, watchin' history repeat itself. Not Arthur and Starr, but Ian and Miss Belle. Ah, but don't they make the perfect pair, Starr? Look at 'em!"

Belle had come to Ian, who held out his hand to her. He caressed her very much like Arthur often caressed me. The game was over. Ian had won my Belle's heart and she, his. I knew Mr. O'Leary would not be taking Belle anywhere with him. Ian Howard would have possession of Belle. I suppose this Ian would be all right for my Belle. Arthur was right about one thing. They looked perfect together.

I nuzzled Arthur, my attitude appreciative now and my maternal instincts quieted to a contented acceptance. As usual, Arthur sensed the change in me—*this man knows me like a book!* He slapped me on the rump familiarly and opened the stall door.

"Come along, my sweet lady," he said. "Let's get you and that filly of yours an apple or two. I think Mr. Howard is gonna make us an offer we can't refuse!"

Ian Howard and Belle met us as we neared the back pasture.

"Mr. Irvin, you have the most beautiful horses in the whole state! Starr and Belle are best of the best! I'll take them both if you're selling!"

I looked with some trepidation at Arthur. I had hardly had a kind thought about him all afternoon. And he knew it.

"No, Master Ian, there's no partin' Starr and me. Besides, Belle there is just like her—you'll have enough just keepin' her! But I guarantee you she'll be a treasure for you, just like Belle here is for me."

I breathed a sigh of relief. I was letting go of Belle, but I would be holding tight to Arthur. Crooked nose, silly glasses, missing teeth and all. I gave my spirited daughter a loud whinny and nudged Arthur to hurry. I was feeling better already!

As Arthur is so fond of saying: There's nothing like a good apple to sweeten a sour mare!

CHAPTER 5

Justus

Place me like a seal over your heart, like a seal on your arm. . .
—Song of Songs 8:6 NIV

I reflect on this impending rendezvous with Olivia with a mixture of anticipation and resignation. I've always looked forward to being with her; I would like to spend every day with her. But I know that's not going to happen. I've always known it, but it's really come home to me recently. Especially now that there is another in her life. He will be the one to fill her thoughts and hold her close at night. I know it just as surely as I'm sitting here in "our" favorite restaurant.

It's not a restaurant, really. Just a fast-food stop with spotless counters and not-so-spotless tables. Bubbly children scatter noisily around the room. Made-in-China plastic toys and made-in-America fast food litter the tables. The parents accompanying the giggling, carefree children look like they need a bed more than a burger. Their smiles are tiredly indulgent. The expressions of other patrons range from oblivious concentration on a newspaper to attentiveness with a luncheon companion.

Me? I'm sitting alone in a mental turmoil of agitation, remembrances, and prayer. Once again I'm waiting and watching for Olivia's arrival.

We used to come here together—just the two of us. I can't help but smile with the memory. That's why we nicknamed this particular place "Justus." For so many years I've called her or she me to meet here. After a time or two we shortened our "Will it be just us?" to one word.

"Justus, Olivia?" I'd say when she answered the telephone.

"Justus for sure!" she would rejoin.

And we would meet, just the two of us, here in our own private world, for minutes or hours to share more than food. It was our special time and special place. Perhaps it was a trifle silly, but we never shared it with anyone else. Neither of us ever came here with anyone else. It was "Justus," Joseph and Olivia, or not at all. *I remember those times so clearly, Lord. I know my praying even now is a jumble of mind-wandering, musing, and entreaty. I just can't seem to get and stay focused. But for so long it has been just the two of us. Now. . .now it looks like it is all coming to an abrupt, painful halt.*

Things started to change about a year or so ago. At first the change was almost imperceptible. Our weekly time together became once every ten days or two weeks. Then it would be three weeks or even a month. She would come to my place—sometimes stay for a few days, but I missed the times here for some strange reason I can't explain. For so long "Justus" has been our secret alone. I'm sure she never divulged it to anyone. I never have! It's been part of our secret bond. Perhaps this bond is about to end. I have a gut-wrenching feeling it is.

My almost-cold coffee and wristwatch both tell me another thing has changed. In recent months she's often been late for our "Justus" times. Once she forgot entirely. I was crushed. The worst of it was that she hadn't even realized she had forgotten until I stopped by her house later that week to deliver her birthday gift. She had met me at the door with a surprised smile and then a gasp.

"Justus! I forgot all about Justus last week, didn't I?"

I waved if off as if it had been nothing. But it had not been nothing. I knew then that our relationship was changing, that "Justus" was becoming a thing of the past. I'll be taking a backseat—no, a ride on the bumper—in Olivia's life from now on. I know it as sure as I'm sitting here. Our lives are changing and things are never going to be the same again. "Justus" is past. And it's because another man has come into her life.

I know I can't compete, Lord. Aaron is everything I'm not. He came into Olivia's life with all the glamour and drama of a Prince Charming on a white horse. As I recall, that was exactly how Olivia had come to know Aaron. She was out horseback riding. I begged off that day for some reason I can't remember. Aaron had come along, his horse not white, but a beautiful, sleek Arabian on which he sat, tall, handsome, and confident. At the moment when Olivia had come riding up, a new companion by her side, I knew this was the beginning of something that did not include me. When Olivia shyly introduced us, I had a sinking feeling in the pit of my stomach.

I didn't miss the sparkle in Olivia's eyes, Lord, as she looked at Aaron who politely made conversation with me. That sparkle had once been for me. As I recall, the longer stretches between our "Justus" sessions began in earnest with the arrival of Aaron Metzger. And it seems to me, Father God, Olivia became more remote.

Does she share secrets with Aaron that once she shared with me alone? When I spend days out of town on business, is Aaron her constant companion? Has she left intimacy with me for. . . ?

"I made it!"

"Olivia! I didn't even see you come in." She pushes her sunglasses up on top of her chocolate-colored hair and gives me a quick kiss on the cheek.

"I'm famished! The traffic gets worse all the time! We're going to have to stop meeting here!" She looks up at the menu and quickly orders. I'm following her around wordlessly like a pathetic, lost puppy. "You're going to have more than coffee, aren't you, Jojo?"

Jojo. She's been calling me that for so long! She's the only one who calls me that. We've been Jojo and Olee for so long. Our private nicknames for each other. Silly. Private. Just ours. Like "Justus." All of a sudden the traffic is a hassle for her. It's been a hassle for years! For years! But now, she has noticed it. Is this going to be the excuse for the end of "Justus"?

"Sure I'm going to have more than coffee!" I reply with more enthusiasm than I feel. "I've been working up an appetite waiting for you. I didn't have breakfast this morning." I order and in a minute we are seated again at our usual table. *Forgive me, Lord, for asking a blessing over this food so mechanically.* I take a tasteless bite of my sandwich. Olivia dives into her sandwich with abandon and continues to talk around bites.

"So how was the latest trip out of town? Do anything fun? Do any running?"

"It was fine. Saw an old business acquaintance I haven't seen in years. We did some catching up and played some handball. I did go running twice, so I didn't spend all my time cooped up in the motel between meetings. What did you do while I was gone?"

"Not much. As you well know without my saying so, my load at school this semester is so heavy that I don't have time to do much more than study. The folks think I've become a recluse."

Between devouring her food and drinking her beverage, she continues talking about her past few weeks while I take in every part of her face. She couldn't have been studying *all* the time; she has that raccoon look from her sunglasses. The pink of her nose and cheeks accents the whiteness of her skin around her hazel eyes. I shift uncomfortably. I'm becoming a self-centered oaf! Why should she go into seclusion just because I'm out of town? She does have a life outside of "Justus." I'm being selfish and stupid to think otherwise. And suddenly I'm feeling very old. . . .

But my life is so wrapped up in hers! And now, it seems, hers is no longer intricately woven to mine. For so long I was the center of her world! Her whole face would become radiant when we had our shared times together. But, whether she admits it in so many words or not, it's clear that Aaron has become the sun for this vital, sparkling woman before me. I, Joseph, have become the shadow. She has never said it—perhaps she has never thought it! But I can read it in her expression when she speaks Aaron's name, as she's now doing.

"What, Olee? I couldn't hear what you said over that little fellow's bellowing." That was a lie. I did hear it, but my attention is all inward.

"I said, 'Aaron passed his bar exam!' It's too bad you're not an attorney, Jojo. You could make him a partner!"

Sure I could, I think to myself. *And hire the attorney general as our third.* The one would be as likely as the other would. But I only smile and nod. Olivia stops talking for a moment and turns all her attention to the last of her sandwich. I drink the last of my bitterly cold coffee and discreetly push the remainder of my food aside.

It's time. A change is coming. Today we've come to a crossroads in our relationship. *Though I'm no prophet, Lord, I can sense it coming.* I can see it in the way she avoids my eyes and the way she keeps scratching one spot just behind her left ear. I learned that nervous habit of hers long ago. I knew things were changing—that they had changed. And today marks the end of what we have so happily called "Justus" for so many years. I wish I could think of something to say to prevent her from saying what I do not want to hear.

"Jojo, I need to tell you something," she says quietly, her eyes at last locking on mine.

Here it comes, Lord. But I only reply, "This is the time and place. After all, it's. . ."

"'Justus,'" she says, finishing my sentence. I reach over to take her hand and give it a meaningful squeeze.

"Aaron has asked me to marry him," she says, barely above a whisper.

So there it is. I'm out—like an old pair of shoes—and Aaron, God bless him, is in. Just like that. No apology, no warning, no explanation. So, what about us and what we've shared?

"I suppose you said 'yes,' " is what I reply, keeping emotion out of my voice.

"I suppose I did!" she says with a giggle, giving my hand a squeeze in return. She grows serious now, her look of quiet delight pulls at me, demanding I enjoy this with and for her. But I cannot. "He's so right for me," she continues. "I knew it the day we met." Her eyes beg me to understand.

"So where is old Jojo going to fit in?" I ask, knowing that I sound like a petulant child. I feel as though I'm being left behind.

"Where Jojo has always fit in," she says emphatically. "Right in the center of my life! Just because I hate the traffic coming over here doesn't mean this still won't be our secret hideaway! I gripe about it, but I'll keep fighting the traffic to get here."

"But there will be no more overnight visits at my house," I say reflectively, grasping for the slightest hope of somehow keeping connected to her.

"That goes without saying, Jojo!" She laughs. "But I'll wager it won't be too long and you'll have another lady sitting across from you here!"

I shrug, not completely catching her meaning, nor wanting to. I will never share "Justus" with anyone else! She might, but I never will. That is all there is to it.

"Nobody else can ever have 'Justus,' " she says, as if reading my mind. "'Justus' is for just Jojo and Olee. Always has been and always will be. In fact, I'm disappointed because we don't do this as much as we used to. I suppose it was your job always taking you out of town."

I know my face showed my astonishment at her words. It hadn't been me! It had been her who had let the lapses invade our times together. Why, I have never. . . !

"But life goes on, doesn't it?" She pauses. "I guess we both let it slip a little," she adds, rubbing her forefinger over my knuckles and giving me space to think. "But no more! I'll need you more than ever. I told you once you were my best friend in the world. That hasn't changed. Nope," she says with a smile that brings both pain and joy to my heart. "There's no end to 'Justus.' We're just getting warmed up! This is just *us*. Nobody else. Not even Aaron. Deal?" she asks, raising her hand to shake mine.

I clasp her soft hand in my own, my heart somewhat lighter than it has been. *Thank You, Lord, for this beautiful young woman who sits before me. Forgive me for my selfishness.*

"Deal," I agree with a calm that has been lacking in my mind for too long. I hesitate only briefly. "Have I told you recently that I love you, Olee?"

"Not since the last time we were here, Jojo."

"Well, I do, my darling Olivia."

"And I love you too, Grandpa. Always have. Always will."

CHAPTER 6

Rocky Too

*"Unless you change and become like little children,
you will never enter the kingdom of heaven."*
—Matthew 18:3 NIV

"What would you like to drink, sir?" The flight attendant reached past Gil Stewart to place a steaming cup of black coffee on the tray in front of his traveling companion.

"Nothing, thanks. I've had plenty. Gonna catch some shut-eye before we touch down in New York." Gil closed his laptop computer and placed it on the floor of the aircraft. He was always glad the company flew him first-class for these interminable overseas flights. His long legs had felt like pretzels the few times he had had to fly coach for stateside trips. He pushed the button to adjust his seat to a reclining position. He would try to get a head start on the inevitable jet lag he would be recovering from during the next two days. He closed his eyes after a glance at his watch.

He was eager to get home. He and his six-year-old son had just moved into a house in a new school district and Gil was feeling guilty for having left Bradley on his own in a new environment. Gil's younger sister had come to the rescue of the two bachelors by telling Gil she would stay with Brad the three weeks he would be in Great Britain. The house wasn't brand-new and Gil suspected Emily would take advantage of his absence to do some redecorating. She was good at that sort of thing and knew his tastes. He'd given her carte blanche to do whatever she thought necessary to make the place more to his liking. He'd purchased it for both its great location and the floor plan, which was exactly what he'd wanted. However, the color scheme and some of the flowery wallpaper had to go. That he left to her and was sure he wouldn't be disappointed. He just hoped it was all done. He didn't feel like living in reconstruction after spending three weeks in a hotel. Gil was sure Emily and Brad would do a good job with the entire undertaking. Bradley had had some definite ideas for his room, including a racing car painted on the one wall. Almost to scale, the thing would dominate the whole room, Gil was sure. As sleep continued to elude him, he thought of Brad.

His son looked a lot like his mother: honey-colored hair and hazel eyes. Lisa had died when Brad was one. Gil still recalled the agony of those first few years after the accident. He didn't think the two of them would ever make it through those toddler years, let alone the incredible loneliness and grief. But they had, and here they were, still chugging along together five years later.

Gil wanted to remarry. He'd been dating off and on for over a couple of years, but he simply couldn't find the woman he thought would be a good mother for Brad. There had been one or two that he thought would be good for *him,* but somehow things never worked out. Maybe he would give Melinda a call once he was back in town again. She was one classy woman and had a great figure. She had come on pretty strong their first date. He just wasn't comfortable moving so fast, so he'd left quickly and kept their subsequent dates earlier, lighter, and with Brad and Melinda's daughter, Tisha, with them. Melinda had started hinting she wanted more than casual dates. She was getting harder to resist. He wasn't quite sure why he *was* resisting getting more intimate with her. *Maybe it's time to stop putting her off and let come what may,* he thought.

Brad seemed to like her. But he wasn't too enamored with Tisha. Gil had to admit he wasn't either. The kid was a tyrant! Brad made friends quickly with boys and girls alike—he was an easy kid to get along with. But he didn't get along with Tisha.

Gil was glad to hear from his son during their telephone calls over the last weeks about his new friends in the neighborhood. *Let's see,* he thought to himself, *there's Ricky, Bruce, Rocky, and Danny.* It sounded as though Brad was adjusting well. He seemed especially taken with this Danny fellow and his dog, Rocky. Neither Brad nor Emily gave Gil much information about Brad's new friends. Brad would just ramble on with a rundown of activities like: "Bruce and I went biking today" or "Danny let me take Rocky for a run" or "Danny and Emily and me went swimming." Even Emily would only say things like "You'll meet Danny when you get home—and Rocky and Ricky and everyone else." Danny, she said, was older than Brad, but Ricky and Bruce were within a year of his age. "Just hurry home and you'll meet everybody, big brother," she had said with a laugh.

Something doesn't sound quite right about this Danny kid somehow. Gil wasn't particularly fond of dogs either—especially big ones which, apparently, Rocky was. Well, he would deal with Rocky and the rest once he got back home. He just knew he was eager to see his son and be home. It wasn't unusual for his telephone conversations with Brad to end up with a tearful: "When are you coming home, Daddy?" which pained Gil. He swore he'd never allow the company to make him take such a long trip again. If Bradley had a mother, it might be different. But this three weeks apart stuff was too much—for Brad and for him.

As Gil thought of home and tried to sleep, his sister Emily and his son Bradley were just as eagerly awaiting his arrival. Brad dried the last dish and set it on the counter from his perch on the chair. Emily finished wiping up the kitchen table.

"Do you think Daddy will like Dani?" Brad asked his aunt for the third time that day and about the hundredth time that week.

"I think so, Brad. Everybody seems to like her—even grouchy Mr. Colgate." Emily smiled at her nephew. "You sure do like her, don't you?"

"She's fun! And she lets me play with Rocky all the time! I wish Dad would let me have a dog. Do you think there's any way we can get him to like Dani and Rocky like we do?" He turned his big eyes on Emily with a searching look.

"I don't think we'll have to do a thing, Bradster. When Dani gets back from her visit to her grandma's we'll have him meet her and Rocky. I think your dad will like them both." *At least I hope he'll like Dani,* she thought to herself. Bradley went off to his room to get ready for their trip to the airport.

Emily looked about the kitchen. She was sure Gil would like the changes she had made. He might not like the size of his charge card balance, but he had told her she could do what she thought was needed. And the house had needed a lot, to her way of thinking. She was especially pleased with the family room. She could visualize Gil and Dani snuggled up on the couch together, eating a bowl of popcorn and enjoying an old movie. She was in agreement with Brad: It was time Gil eased up on his hours at work and got himself a wife and Bradley a mother! And Danielle Sheppard was the perfect person for both positions!

As soon as Emily met Dani, she knew she was the one for Gil. Dani and Gil had many of the same interests, not the least of which was Bradley. Dani seemed to enjoy a special friendship with all the kids in the neighborhood, but she and Brad had hit it off marvelously from the very first. It was Brad who wanted to keep Dani's identity a secret from his dad, however. They thought it would be more fun this way—just plop Dani right in front of him! *How could he resist those long eyelashes and big dimples?* Emily thought with a mischievous smile.

She had decided God had miraculously kept these two from anybody else so they would end up together. God probably didn't need her help or Brad's, but they'd make sure things got started in the right direction before Gil had time to call that Melinda woman and her monster kid, Tisha. Emily shuddered to think her brother would ever even consider dating that sleazy Melinda.

"Hurry up, Cupid!" she called up the stairs. "Let's go get Dani's Prince Charming before he decides we're not coming and calls a cab!"

"Who's Cupid?" Bradley asked, pulling on a ball cap.

"I'll tell you some other time. Are you ready?" she asked, grabbing her keys and purse.

"Should we tell Daddy about Dani? I mean, that she's a girl and everything?" he asked as they left the house.

"No, let's just try to keep it a secret a little longer, okay?" she asked.

"I hope Daddy likes Rocky and Dani, Aunt Emily," he said once more, snapping his seat belt.

"I hope so, too." She didn't want Brad getting his hopes set on their new friend too much. She was a bit younger than the women Gil had occasionally dated. *Maybe Gil will think she's too young.* Emily hadn't considered that before.

"I've been praying about it, like you said," Brad replied as they made their way to the airport. He turned to her with a bright smile. "I can't wait to see Dad!" he said. "It seems like he's been gone a *long* time!"

"It sure does," she agreed. "Wait till he sees your new haircut! And your room! I bet he'll really like it!" she assured him.

"I hope he can stay home with us for a while. I don't want him goin' to work," he said, his face suddenly drawn up into a pout.

Me too, Emily said to herself, but just smiled at her nephew.

Gil had not expected his meeting at the airport with Emily and Brad to be so emotional. He thought his son looked three inches taller and a year older. He barely kept the tears back as he picked Brad up and returned his clinging hug. Gil gave Emily a quick kiss on the cheek as he continued to hold his son tightly.

"Have you two managed to keep the new place together? Emily hasn't burned it down with her cooking, has she, Brad?" he asked, winking at his sister.

"Nah. We ate burgers out a lot," Brad said innocently, still holding tightly to his father's neck.

"That is not true, Bradley Stewart, and you know it!" Emily said with mock anger, reaching to pinch his bottom.

"No, it's not. . .we went out for pizza and tacos too!" he announced.

"This kid of yours is incorrigible, did you know that?" she asked Gil good-naturedly. Brad laughed and buried his face against Gil's chest.

"Takes after his Aunti Em," Gil retorted, laughing in turn.

"I'm all ready for school, Dad. Aunt Emily took me to get some new clothes. You have to take me to get pencils and school stuff. I've got a soccer game Friday. We won last week! I almost scored a goal too! Mr. Dulinsky took us for ice cream after the game. I got some mosquito bites on my arm. See?" Brad stopped talking briefly to twist his arm around at an angle for his father to see the red marks.

"Why didn't you put some spray on?" Gil asked, reluctantly setting his son down so he could walk with them himself.

"We couldn't find it. Aunt Emily bought me some more. Wait till you see my room, Dad! It looks so neat! Bruce wants Aunt Emily to draw a car on his wall too! Ricky's mom and dad got a new pool and we've been swimming in it almost every day!"

Bradley continued his excited monologue and Gil enjoyed every second of it. He was so glad just to listen to and touch his son again that he didn't think he'd ever tire of his chatter. He and Emily kept smiling over Brad's bobbing head, as she would confirm with a nod or a shrug to his one-sentence tales. By the time the three of them had picked up Gil's tennis racquet and luggage, and they had made their way to the car, Bradley was talking less, but was still clinging to his father's hand.

"Me and Aunt Emily—" Brad began.

"Aunt Emily and I," his father corrected.

"Aunt Emily and me have been goin' to Dani and Ricky's church, Dad," Brad said as they started for home.

"Is that so?" Gil asked, kicking off his shoes and glad for Emily's offer to drive.

"Yeah. Almost everyone in my class goes to my school too. We start soon. Aunt Emily has been helping me practice some letters and stuff." Bradley began a close scrutiny of the assortment of miniature vehicles Gil had purchased for him during his trip. He raised his head to look at his dad from the backseat. "You don't have to go to work today, do you, Dad?"

"No, son. I won't go in today or tomorrow. I wanted to have

some time with you and Aunt Emily before she has to go home and get ready for her last year of college. We've got to finish getting everything ready for you for school too." He didn't mention that it would probably take him the better part of a day just to sort through all his E-mail. Technology had its drawbacks, especially when you were out of the country for a while. His sister seemed to read his mind.

"Just make sure you're not sitting at your computer for a straight ten hours tomorrow," she said for his ears only. She brushed her hand through her dark, shoulder-length hair and glanced in the rearview mirror at her nephew. "We fixed you something real special for supper tonight, didn't we, Brad?"

"Oh, yeah! I was just joking before, Dad. Aunt Emily can cook okay," he said, engrossed with his new toys.

"You can't imagine how much I'm looking forward to a home-cooked meal!" Gil said. "I don't want to see the inside of a restaurant for a month!"

Gil enjoyed walking through the house, Brad chattering away beside him, and Emily apologizing for the cost of everything she had purchased. Gil was pleased with it all and casually waved off his sister's apologies. He was home! He took a shower and put on some jeans and a comfortable T-shirt. The new carpeting felt good on his bare feet and he decided to swear off shoes for the next couple of days as well. It would be bare feet or sandals! The wing tips and loafers could rot in the closet! He and Brad wrestled on the family room floor while Emily finished the last of the supper preparations.

"All right, you two!" she announced. "Time to wash those hands and come and eat!"

Red-faced and laughing, Gil flipped Brad on his stomach and laid himself over his son.

"Surrender! Surrender or I'll flatten you like a pancake!" Gil said, holding his wiggling son's body beneath his own.

"I give up!" Brad yelled, giggling. "I give up!"

Gil rolled off him and laid flat, his arms outstretched on the carpet. Bradley quickly jumped up and sat down with a plop on his father's stomach. A big "oomph!" emanated from Gil and he pulled his son down against his chest.

"All right, already!" Emily spoke more loudly and commandingly this time. "You're home together less than two hours and you're destroying the place! Enough! Wash your hands!" She made to hit Bradley's bottom with the large plastic spoon in her hand as he rolled off his father and scrambled to the bathroom.

"Whew! I needed that!" Gil declared, stretching out once again and slowing pulling himself up to his full six-foot-four frame.

"Not to mention another shower!" his sister quipped. "At least wash your hands and face. You look like you've been in the hot sun for a week!" She went back to the kitchen and Gil went to wash up. He used his hands to brush the hair back out of his eyes and noted he would need to get to the barber's soon. His naturally curly hair was almost in his eyes and more than halfway down his neck. He had shaved, but he thought he still looked like a kid who was sporting long hair just to rattle anyone with a more conservative bent.

"Oh well," he mumbled to himself. "You're not going to be meeting anyone tonight. Don't need to worry about making a bad impression." He quickly washed his hands and splashed off his face.

As Gil made his way to the kitchen, the doorbell rang. He shooed Bradley to the kitchen with a wave of his hand and called over his shoulder to Emily.

"I'll get it!"

Gil opened the door to a young woman dressed in a short top and brightly colored running shorts. She had a ball cap on her head. Her long blond braid stuck out from the back of the ball cap and went almost to her waist. Her eyes were hidden behind shiny, reflective sunglasses and she had in-line skates on. A powerfully built Akita stood beside her. The dog regarded Gil without any eager tail-wagging. The young woman's engaging smile immediately disappeared. She pulled off her sunglasses and they hung around her neck by a sports chain. The darkest, longest eyelashes Gil had ever seen surrounded her pale blue eyes. She was strikingly attractive and slender. He couldn't get over the contrast her eyelashes made between the lightness of her eyes and her flawless complexion.

"Oh. . .hi!" she said, somewhat awkwardly. "Is Emily or Bradley here?"

"Dani! Rocky!" Brad exclaimed, suddenly materializing out of nowhere, right next to Gil. He quickly pushed his way around the screen door and embraced the Akita, whose tail was now wagging earnestly. The smile came back to the woman's face as she reached her hand down to Brad's head. Gil noticed the deep dimples on either side of her smile.

"Hi, Bradster! We just got back and thought you and Emily might want to ride your bikes with us. I didn't know your dad was home." She turned her incredible eyes back on Gil and held out her hand. "Brad's dad, I presume?" she asked, not waiting for an answer. "I'm Danielle Sheppard—the neighbor from next door."

"Hi, Dani! You're back!" Emily came up beside Gil. "Has Brad introduced you?"

"Well, I was just in the process of introducing myself, Em. I'm sorry I got you at a bad time. I forgot you were coming home today, Mr. Stewart," she said by way of apology.

"Can Dani and Rocky have supper with us, Dad?" Brad asked from his position on the porch, his arm draped over Rocky. Gil didn't have a minute to answer.

"Oh, no, Brad. We'll get together later. You go ahead and have supper. I'll call you later, Emily," Dani said and started to back off the porch.

"Come back and join us for dessert, why don't you?" Emily asked, without looking at her brother. "Go ahead and skate and then come back when you're done, okay?"

"I don't think I should," Dani began.

"Can she, Dad?" piped up Brad. "And Rocky too? He does all kinds of neat tricks!"

Gil felt Emily poke him in the back. "Uh. . .sure. Why don't you join us? I've heard a lot about you and Rocky," Gil said. *I sure didn't hear the most important thing,* he thought to himself. *A little older than Brad, eh, Emily?* That was the year's *biggest* understatement! Gil thought Dani might be close to Emily's age of twenty-two—maybe twenty-four at most. Not to mention she wasn't the type of "Danny" he'd expected.

Dani continued to move away from them with the Akita in tow. "If you're sure it won't be any trouble," she said. She pulled her sunglasses back up and skated towards the driveway for the street.

"No trouble at all!" Emily said, smiling. "Come on, Brad. They'll be back," she said, opening the door wider for Bradley to come back in the house.

Emily secretly gave a thumbs-up sign to Bradley as Gil watched their unexpected guest disappear around the corner. Brad grinned at his aunt with raised eyebrows and walked with her back towards the kitchen.

When Gil sat down at the table with his sister and son, he was surprised to have Brad reach for his hand, as well as his aunt's.

"We've been praying before we eat, Dad," Bradley announced. "Aunt Emily and Dani taught me."

"Oh," was all Gil could respond to this bit of news. He followed his son's lead and bowed his head while Brad prayed. He didn't know what to make of this new development.

"Thank You, Jesus, for bringing Daddy home. Thank You for this food. Thank You for Rocky. Amen."

Gil was touched, but also looked questioningly at his sister as he raised his head. She was not looking at him (he suspected) purposely. She began dishing out the casserole she had made. Gil wondered if she had been talking to Brad a lot about her religion. He wondered too if this Dani was religious like Emily. He decided to ask Brad.

"Why have you started praying before eating, Brad?" he asked gently, keeping his tone conversational while dishing some vegetables onto his son's plate.

"After Sunday school class last week I prayed with Dani and asked Jesus into my heart," his son answered. "She teaches my Sunday school class."

"I see," Gil said, giving Emily a "we'll talk about this later" look. He wasn't a churchgoer himself. He and God weren't exactly on speaking terms since his wife's death.

"We studied all about how Jesus fed a bunch of people with some goldfish and bread. I don't know why anybody would eat goldfish!" Brad shook his head as he filled his mouth with some food.

"Jesus fed people *goldfish?*" Gil asked Emily.

"Well, I don't think it was goldfish," she replied with a smile. "Probably some kind of smoked something-or-other from the Sea of Galilee." She turned to her nephew. "Brad, don't drink all your milk or you won't finish your food."

"You'll like Dani's church, Dad," Brad continued, setting

down his almost-empty glass of milk. "They do some fun things there."

Since when was church fun? Gil wanted to know, but he'd save that question for later too.

"Isn't Dani pretty, Dad? And isn't Rocky the neatest dog you've ever seen? Can I get a dog? I'd feed him and everything!"

"We'll see," was all Gil said before he changed the subject.

Two hours later Dani came back. *With the dog,* Gil noted with some chagrin. The Akita still regarded him warily as he came downstairs. Gil wondered if there was any polite way to ask Dani to leave the dog at home next time. Or at least tie him up outside. He didn't relish the thought of dog hair all over the new carpet. Brad was already dancing excitedly around the dog as Emily and Dani talked. Brad looked up as his dad entered the living room.

"Want to see Rocky's tricks, Dad? He obeys me just like he does Dani!" Without waiting a reply, he stepped back from the dog. "Rocky, sit." Rocky sat.

"Rocky, play dead," Brad commanded. Rocky let out a quiet whine, lay down, and was as still as a stone. Brad grinned up at his dad. "Watch this, Daddy," he said, turning again to the Akita.

"Rocky, protect!"

The dog jumped up, stood between Brad and his father, and bared his teeth with a low growl as he faced Gil. He could have sworn the dog looked pleased to be in the "protect" mode. *The only thing that would please the mutt more would be to take a piece out of my backside,* he thought.

"Rocky, come," Dani interrupted. The dog came to stand beside her. She gently scolded Bradley. "Don't ever do that with your dad or any of your friends, Brad! That's only for when you're in danger. Rocky doesn't know you're kidding." She snapped her fingers and Rocky sat beside her, no longer snarling or growling, but still regarding Gil with watchful vigilance. Gil was doing some of his own watchful vigilance. He decided he didn't trust the dog. He didn't like him much either. Obviously, the feeling was mutual.

"Sorry, Mr. Stewart—"

"Please. It's Gil," he said. "Well, Gil to you. Mr. Stewart to Rocky there," he added, nodding in the dog's direction.

"Would you like me to tie him up outside?" Dani asked.

"He's fine, Dani," Emily answered for her brother. "He can sit in the kitchen while we have our dessert." The roll of Gil's eyes was lost on his sister.

The five of them went to the kitchen, Brad giving Rocky the command to "heel," which meant Gil followed at a bit of a distance, not sure Rocky wouldn't spontaneously jump back into his "protect" posture. Gil offered to get the beverages while Emily started cutting the pie.

Bradley certainly seems smitten with Dani, Gil thought. He'd be hard-pressed to figure who Brad liked better: the attractive blond or the performing dog. He noted the way Dani looked at his son. *Tenderly. Lovingly. Motherly.*

"Ouch!" He barely set the cup down before dropping it. *Where had* that *thought come from?*

"You okay, klutz?" Emily giggled, reaching for the washcloth.

"What?" he stammered. "Uh, yeah. Just got distracted for a second and wasn't watching where I was pouring. . ." When he looked up, he noticed Dani regarding him with her beautiful eyes. She looked down quickly. Gil was sure she blushed. She turned her attention quickly back to Brad who had begun chattering to her again as he showed her the cars Gil had bought for him.

"Dani, do you take cream or sugar?" he asked, trying to

clear his head of words like "motherly." What had come over him? Hadn't he just been thinking about Melinda earlier in the day? He concluded it must be the jet lag playing havoc with his brain.

"Just black, thanks," she said, her attention back on Bradley.

While Dani was engaged with the talkative Brad and his cars, Gil cast a sidelong glance at Rocky, who was silently staring at him. *If you think you're getting so much as a drop of water from me, you point-eared cur, you can forget it!* Gil thought with a glare at the dog. He wondered if the beast could read minds as well as play dead. Gil was sure he saw Rocky's upper lip curl up slightly, showing some rather large white teeth.

The telephone rang and Emily set down the knife she was using on the pie. "I'll get it in the other room," she said.

"Hello. Stewarts'," Emily said as she picked up the phone.

"Hi. Is Gil there?" asked a breathy voice. Emily knew it was Melinda.

"Yes, he is," she replied, "but we have company right now. She and Gil are busy." She paused to let that sink in for a minute. "May I take a message or have him call you back?" she asked sweetly. There was a pause on the other end of the line.

"Well, um. . ." the caller stammered. "I. . .would you ask him to call Melinda? He can call as late as he wants—I'll be up for a while. In fact," her voice sounded bolder now, "have him call me as soon as he's free."

"Why don't you give me your number?" Emily asked.

"He knows it. Just give him the message." There was a click and then the familiar drone of the phone line.

Emily looked at the receiver before putting it down. She wrote the message down, hoping Gil wouldn't ask who called. He did. . .as soon as she returned to the kitchen.

"Who was that, Em?" he asked, setting a glass of milk in front of Bradley.

"One of your coworkers. I wrote down the name and message next to the phone," she answered, hoping that would pacify him for the moment. She hadn't told Dani about Melinda. She had only told her Gil was good-looking, responsible, a loving father, a lonely widower, and needed someone to keep him closer to home more often. She had not told Dani that Gil didn't like dogs. She thanked God secretly that she had limited her comments to the truth. *The dog might prove a problem in our matchmaking here,* she thought. For his part, Gil appeared to accept her vague response and sat down at the table with Dani and Brad.

"This is great peach pie, Em!" he said. "Mom's recipe?"

"Actually," she purred, "it's Dani's recipe. The only thing she does better than baking is beat me at tennis!"

"Oh! You're a tennis buff, Danielle?" he asked. Before she could do much more than nod, Brad answered for her.

"She can do lots of things, Dad! She can play catch good—"

"Well," Gil corrected.

"She can dive. She's been teaching me how to dive off the diving board! She can sing, she's a nurse, and she teaches my Sunday school class," Brad enthused, parking one of his toy cars on his plate next to his piece of pie.

"So you told me," Gil said.

"Dani and Aunt Emily went to all my games while you were gone. Are you going to go with us tomorrow for my game?" he asked.

"Of course I'm going to your game!" Gil responded.

"You can ride over with us," Emily said offhandedly to Dani.

"Oh, I don't think—" Dani began.

"You're not going to stop going to my games now that Dad's home, are you, Dani?" Bradley asked. Emily noted Gil's attention on the embarrassed smile Dani directed at him.

"Well, Brad, your Aunt Emily is going to be going home soon. And now that your dad is home, I don't think you need me to—"

"Hey! The more people Brad's team has rooting for them, the more likely they'll be to win! You're welcome to join us," Gil reiterated. He took a drink of coffee.

"It's settled then!" Emily said with a small, but knowing smile. "We'll all do the game tomorrow!"

Soon after they finished their dessert, Dani and Rocky went home. Gil's flight across time zones was catching up with him and his yawns were becoming more frequent. Emily offered to tuck Brad in for the night when Gil ascended the steps for bed at eight o'clock. Gil was so tired he didn't ask Emily any of the questions he had earlier. He never glanced at the message pad next to the telephone, which secretly pleased Emily. She was going to do everything in her power to keep Melinda away from her brother. She simply didn't like the woman. She hung on Gil like a leech. Emily decided to give Dani a call once she had put Bradley to bed.

"Well," she began unceremoniously, "what do you think of him? I mean, you have to overlook the fact that he's been up almost thirty-six hours, so he's not at his best."

"He seems nice, Em," was Dani's short reply.

"Nice? That's all you've got to say?" Emily asked, throwing her hands up in exasperation.

"What did you want me to say?" Dani asked. "He's good-looking, like you said, he seems wonderful with Brad. . . . What else?" She hesitated. "He barely looked at me, Emily," she said quietly.

"Are you kidding? He's half-asleep and hasn't seen his son in almost a month! *I* would say he was doing his best not to look at you! He was afraid of love at first sight," she said firmly.

"Sure. Listen, I've got to get going, Em. I have to finish up Sunday's lesson and I work day shift tomorrow. I'll call you when I get home." The two new friends hung up after their good-byes. Emily sat in the chair, planning her next course of action.

It didn't take much planning.

Once Gil woke up, he and Brad went off for the day to buy school supplies and simply spend the day together alone. Emily took another message from the persistent Melinda, telling her that "Gil, the neighbor next door, and Brad had plans for the evening" and that, yes, she would make sure to have Gil call Melinda as soon as he could. Emily received a call from a guy that she had been dating. She accepted his invitation to go to a movie. She had two good reasons for accepting: She really liked this guy, and this would give Gil a chance to spend time with just Dani and Brad. *Perfect,* she thought. *Maybe I can get this romance off the ground before I go home!*

Dani showed up at Gil's promptly at six o'clock. It wasn't until then that Emily announced to all of them that she wouldn't be going to the game. Gil seemed to think nothing of it, Brad gave her a surreptitious smile, and Dani's look was nondescript. The telephone rang just as they started to leave. Emily hoped it wasn't Melinda. Gil answered the telephone.

"Oh, hi, Melinda! I'm sorry I've haven't returned your calls. Brad and I—"

She doesn't even have the courtesy to let the man finish his sentence, Emily thought with a "What should we do now?" look thrown at her nephew. She heard Gil ask Melinda to hold on.

"Dani, if it's not an imposition, would you mind taking Brad after the game?"

"Aw, Dad," Brad groaned before Dani could reply. "I wanted

you to go to this new pizza place with Dani and me after the game. It's really something! Could we?" he asked.

You're doing your aunt proud, little guy, Emily thought. But she only looked on innocently.

"Oh," Gil said, running his fingers through his shaggy hair. "Listen, Melinda. I can't tonight. How about if I call you tomorrow? Tisha will be back from your mom's tomorrow. . . why? Is that a problem? The four of us. . ."

"Maybe we should go out to the car," Dani said quietly to Brad. "Have Gil come on out when he's done on the phone," she said to Emily. Dani and Brad went outside.

"I. . .I'll just call you tomorrow and we can make some plans, okay?" He hesitated. Emily tried to be discreet about listening to the conversation. She busied herself with doing some picking up in the family room.

"No, I don't think I can come by tonight—not even later," she heard Gil say.

What nerve! Emily puffed up a throw pillow with a vengeance. She hoped her brother hadn't been sleeping with Melinda. She knew she couldn't expect much—Gil was not a womanizer, but he had never made a lifetime commitment to Jesus Christ as she had. Emily sincerely hoped he hadn't been with any woman in the days since Lisa's death. She doubted he had; he'd never been too serious with any woman since Lisa. But this Melinda was a manipulative, never-take-no-for-an-answer, high-powered executive who was used to getting what she wanted. And it was clear to Emily that she wanted Gil Stewart.

Over my dead body, Emily fumed. She gave the pillow another vicious punch.

"I'll call you tomorrow. . . . . Yeah, bye," Gil said. Emily breathed a sigh of relief as Gil hung up the telephone.

"They're waiting outside for you. Don't wait up for me!"

she called over her shoulder as she went upstairs to change clothes.

"Sorry to keep you guys waiting," Gil said as he climbed in the car.

Dani had tucked all of her golden hair under her ball cap. A few ringlets hung around her face. As she helped Brad get strapped into the backseat Gil couldn't help looking at her long, tanned legs. He turned to check on Brad himself and noted Rocky's usual, cold stare leveled on him. *Does Dani go anywhere without the beast in tow?* he grumbled silently. Brad draped a skinny arm around the Akita's shoulders.

"Ready to go!" he announced.

"Here. Let me help you with that belt. . . . It gets stuck sometimes." Gil's hand brushed Dani's as he took hold of the seat belt. He could smell her perfume. He had initially invited Dani to the game thinking she'd be a great nanny of sorts for Brad when Emily went home, and Gil wanted to get to know her better on that basis. But now he was thinking less of her as a baby-sitter and more as a possible date. *Get a grip, Stewart,* he told himself. *She's not the first beautiful woman to sit next to you.*

"All ready?" he asked.

"Ready!" Dani and Brad affirmed together. Rocky added his own "woof" as if confirming their response. Gil had to laugh in spite of himself.

Gil hadn't realized how much he had missed Brad's games. He was pleased that Dani was as vocal as he was. The snatches of conversation were brief throughout the game, but Gil took in each opportunity to look into her gorgeous eyes and note the dimples on either side of her perfectly shaped mouth. His recollection of Melinda was getting dimmer by the minute.

"Listen, Dani," he began during a lull in the game. "I'm going to be needing someone to watch Brad before I get home from work some nights. Our moving here and his new full day of school are going to dictate a lot of changes for us. Would your work schedule allow you to watch Brad for me until I can make other arrangements?"

"I don't know. As I told you, I only work on a contingency basis at the hospital. Maybe we can talk about some kind of schedule soon," she replied.

"How about over supper tomorrow? There's a new Greek restaurant across town that I'd like to try." *I can't believe I'm saying this,* he thought. *Eating out* again!

"You're probably tired of eating out after being gone for so long. My folks will be out of town for the weekend, so I'll have the house to myself. Why don't you and Brad come over for supper?"

This girl doesn't miss a thing. He put on his best businesslike smile.

"Since we're going to talk business, how about just the two of us?" he asked. "Emily will be leaving Sunday. I'm sure she wouldn't mind spending a few more hours alone with Brad before she goes." *Besides, I think I would like to have you all to myself for a while.*

He was pleased to see her smile as she pulled off her ball cap and shook her hair out freely. He wanted to touch the silky gold that she lightly separated with her fingers. But he continued to sit, his hands holding onto the edge of the bleacher.

"Okay. But it will be the three of us."

"Rocky too?" he asked, glancing at the dog, who actually looked to be watching the game.

"Rocky too. In fact," she smiled at him, "I may tell you why I always keep him close at hand." She jumped up to cheer for Bradley's team. Gil stood with her, joining in the applause.

I can just guess, he thought, casting another glance at the dog.

Emily could hardly keep from squealing with delight when Gil asked her to screen his calls the next day. "If Melinda calls again," he said quietly, "tell her I'll see her at work Monday. I'm busy the rest of the weekend. Apologize for me, will you?" Emily was more than happy to do so. But she simply smiled demurely and agreed.

After spending the day working in the yard and going over more of his voice mail, Gil stood before the mirror in his room, trying to decide how casually he should dress. He decided to wear a comfortable golf shirt and slacks. He rolled his eyes at himself in the mirror again. The haircut! He forgot to get his hair cut! He looked like a Neanderthal! He stuck his feet in his most comfortable shoes and ran down the stairs. He gave Brad some quick directions for the evening.

"You're gonna go to church with us in the morning, aren't you, Dad?" Brad asked. "It's going to be Aunt Emily's last time before she goes home."

"Well, son, I was thinking of going over to the club for some tennis. . ." He saw Brad's face fall, so decided to cushion his answer. "But we'll see," he ended. *What was this sudden fascination with church?* he wondered. *Of course, if I had had a Sunday school teacher that looked like Dani when I was a kid, I'd probably want to go to church too!*

"Dad," Brad said, "are you gonna kiss Dani tonight?"

Gil almost ran into the wall.

"I. . .uh. . .hadn't thought about it." *That was a lie.* "Why do you ask?" he asked Brad, glad Emily wasn't around at the moment. She seemed to be in some kind of matchmaking mode all of a sudden. Gil preferred to make his own matches.

"Just wondered. She's pretty, isn't she?" Brad asked, turning his concentration back to his toys.

Gil took advantage of Brad's diversion and quietly left the family room, calling up to Emily that he was leaving. She appeared at the top of the stairs.

"Kurt and I are going to take Bradley to the German-American Festival. Just so you know where we are. . ." She gave her brother a smug grin. "Have a good time with Danielle."

Gil didn't know what to expect at Dani's house, but when she answered the door in a simple white summer dress and her bare feet, he was almost speechless. Her simple beauty fired his fast-developing attraction to her. With her customary, easy grace she welcomed him in and he followed her to the kitchen. Her hair, shimmering in the late afternoon sunshine, cascaded down her back in gentle, loose curls.

"Maybe we should go out, Dani," he said. "I didn't know you were going to dress up. . . ."

As if on cue, Rocky appeared at her side, and appraised Gil with his customary *lack* of grace. Dani patted his head and slipped on some sandals that were near the table.

"Quite frankly, my jeans are in the laundry. Besides, this is the most comfortable thing I own. Here, could you take these out onto the deck? It's such a nice evening I thought we should eat outside." She handed him two glasses with ice and indicated the way to the backyard. She picked up a bowl of fruit and the three of them went out. The backyard was spacious and full of flowers and plants. One large oak tree provided them with shade on the deck.

"I hope you don't mind," she said. "I kept it simple: grilled chicken breasts, fruit salad, and a pasta dish." He sat down and poured the lemonade into their glasses as she retrieved the chicken from the grill. "Everything is ready," she said, setting down the plate of chicken and sitting across from him. "I'll pray," she said simply and bowed her head. Gil followed her lead and mumbled an "amen" when she concluded her prayer. He thought that was probably the proper thing to do.

"You've not told me why you still live at home," he began as she served him. "It's so unusual for anyone to live with their folks after college. Em has a great relationship with our folks, but she plans to move out on her own right after graduation."

"Mom has rheumatoid arthritis. She has her good days and bad. Since Dad still works, she needs someone close by to help her on her bad days. So, since my sister has her own family and I'm a nurse, it just naturally falls to me. I pay room and board and enjoy my folks. They do manage to have a fairly busy lifestyle, so sometimes it's like living alone!" She thought a moment and then laughed. "Of course, sometimes it's hardly that at all! It's unusual to have a 'gentleman caller' here without Pop to give him a good going-over."

They talked throughout the course of Dani's delicious meal, getting to know each other more, and enjoying companionable togetherness. Much of their conversation kept coming back to Bradley. Gil thought Dani's eyes sparkled every time she spoke of his son. It was clear she had forged quite an attachment to him in a short time. That made him glad. Melinda had never seemed to have much interest in Brad. He wasn't sure why that came into his head while he was sitting with Dani. He brought his concentration back to her.

"Would you like to take a walk?" she invited. "I could show you around the neighborhood a bit. Show you where the guys hang out—where Brad's best buddies live and all." Gil agreed. "Of course," she said with a coy smile, "Rocky goes too.

Of course, he thought, but only smiled in return.

Gil wasn't quite sure what to make of the church the next morning. It was a big place. He only went to church at Christmas. He, Emily, and Brad sat together with a friend of Brad's joining them after his mother made sure it was all right with Gil. Gil might have felt more out of place than he did, had everyone not been so friendly. Emily and Bradley seemed to know a lot of people for only having been there a few times. Gil decided it was because of Dani, who seemed to know *everybody.*

He met Dani's friend, Gina, and decided he would give her day care center a try. He didn't have many, if any, options at this late date as it was. During the course of the service, Gil was impressed with the preacher. He seemed genuine and straightforward. Some of his comments made Gil uncomfortable and he found it interesting how many people had Bibles. It looked as though many of them were checking up on the preacher to make sure he was quoting it correctly. Gil was about to say something to that effect to Emily when he noticed she seemed to be concentrating on the sermon. So he just kept his thought to himself. He looked over at Dani a few times. She looked great. But her look had something else too. He wasn't sure what it was. Tranquility? Purity? He didn't know. Whatever it was, it only increased his interest in her more. He decided it might have something to do with her being a Sunday school teacher.

After the service was over, he, Emily, and Brad left quickly to help get Emily packed and drive her back home. Gil and his dad played the tennis game Gil had wanted to play all weekend. His mother stuffed Brad full of cookies. It was a day of pure enjoyment for Gil and Brad both. It was late when they got home and it was all Gil could do to get Brad bathed and his teeth brushed before he dropped off to sleep. Gil spent the evening getting ready for his week at work, which he was sure would be a full one. But knowing this would be Brad's first week at school made him promise himself not to get too buried under the load at work.

By Thursday evening Gil was eager for the weekend to arrive. Things had been going well for Bradley at school and there had been no problems with the day care or his arrangements for picking Brad up at a reasonable hour. Bradley was excited about everything. He liked his teacher. He liked his school. His best friends were in his class. The one night Dani had picked him up he had been able to play with Rocky for over an hour. He even enjoyed the day care center. Gil's week had not been so pleasant. He wasn't sure he'd ever catch up from his weeks away from the office. He had at least one three-hour meeting a day and his secretary was out with a sick child at home. To say Melinda was cool toward him would have been an understatement. Her look could freeze butter in the summer sun. After Tuesday he made a point of staying out of her way. The week had been overwhelming and he had taken more aspirin than was probably good for him to keep his headaches at bay. After he had put Brad in bed for the night he fixed himself a chocolate malted and sat out on his front porch.

"Hi! Want some company?" Dani came walking up the street with her father and Rocky.

"Sure. I can get some chairs. . . ." Gil got up to go to the garage, but Dani waved him off. She said something to her dad and he and Rocky continued on their way to their house. Dani walked up the sidewalk and sat on the porch step next to where Gil had been sitting.

"I'll just sit here next to you. Don't get a chair," she said. "Dad's got some project to work on, so don't think he's being unsociable." Gil sat beside her and held up his evening snack.

"Want one? I make a mean chocolate malt," he said.

"No, but thanks, Gil. Brad in bed?" she asked.

"Yeah. How's your week been?"

"Busy. I don't usually work three days straight, but they were desperate, so I've put in more time than I normally do. Mom's had a good week, so it's worked out okay. How about you?"

"Hectic. Harried. Tense. I hope it gets better soon. This resolution of mine to be home more for Brad makes it tough at work. I could be at the office fourteen hours a day and not get everything done." He set his empty glass down beside him and rested his elbows on the porch.

"All the more reason not to then, right?" She turned her eyes on him. He met her look with a smile of his own.

"Right." He thought for a few seconds while they watched a couple walk by. "Brad has a birthday party to go to on Saturday. How about some tennis?"

"That would be nice. What time?"

"I can pick you up after I run Bradley over to Bruce's. . .say, a little after one?"

"Sounds good. I hope you can get the court time."

"To be honest, I already got the time. I figured if you couldn't make it, I'd call one of the guys at work. How about Saturday night? Got any plans?" *I'm on a roll here,* he thought. *Might as well go for the whole enchilada.*

"Well, there was a possibility that I might have a date, but he hasn't called back to confirm it, so yes, I guess I am free." She unclasped her barrette and shook her hair loose.

"I was going to take Brad and a friend of his choice to the university's game. It wouldn't be too late of a night."

"Sounds like fun. We can talk about the time after our match Saturday. Well, suppose I'd better get home," she said, standing to leave. "See you then."

He stood and watched her return to her house, calling a good night when she got to her door. He sat back down. *So, Dani has at least one other interested suitor. Competition.* Gil rubbed the back of his hand across the rough surface of his chin. He sure didn't like this dating stuff. Made him feel like a kid again somehow. Melinda had made it all seem too easy; with Dani he wasn't sure where he stood. Well, he'd only known the woman for a week or so. For now he was going to look forward to Saturday. . .another date with his son's Sunday school teacher. He felt good about that.

After dropping Brad off at his friend's house on Saturday, Gil made a quick return trip home to pick up Dani. She came outside and got into his car before he had time to turn off the ignition. She reminded him of the first time he had met her at his front door—complete with her sunglasses and hair pulled back in a long braid, which she proceeded to wrap around her head.

"Hi! Ready to get beat?" she asked, her dimples deep and her smile wide.

"Don't tell me. You also put yourself through nursing school as a part-time tennis instructor," he said, pulling out onto the street.

"Something like that," she baited, a coy smile between her dimples.

"Oh, brother," he groaned. "My ego isn't about to take a bashing on the court after the week I've had at work, is it?"

"I guess we'll see," she said with a challenging grin.

Their tennis match turned out to be exhilarating for both of them. Gil was the stronger player and server, but Dani had little trouble returning many of his serves and had a backhand that Gil envied from the first time he saw it—and missed it. At the end of the hour they were both breathing hard, wet with perspiration, and eager to get something to drink. They found a spot on the club's veranda that afforded some shade and the benefit of a cooling breeze. After quenching their thirst, Gil went and bought sandwiches for the two of them for a light lunch.

"Mind if I give thanks for the food?" she asked. Gil said no and followed Dani's lead as she bowed her head and then said a brief prayer. They ate in silence for a few seconds.

"You pray about everything?" Gil asked. "Did you pray about our tennis match?"

Dani laughed. "I was going to say 'yes,' but I confess I did not pray about the tennis."

Gil ate some more of his sandwich before continuing. "Why? Why pray about everything? The last time I remember praying was before Lisa died. I was feeling a little overwhelmed. I'm not sure the praying helped much."

"Sometimes God's answers to prayer aren't spectacular or noteworthy. Sometimes it's a matter of simply coming out at the end of it all and realizing: 'I made it.' "

"Hmm. I never thought of it that way before. Of course, I can always come up with some exceptions."

"We can all do that," she conceded. "That's where real faith comes in." She reached down to put her socks and shoes back on. "Thanks for lunch. It was good."

Gil's portable telephone rang and he took a final drink of water. "Hello. . .hi, son. Ready for me to come and get you?" Dani gathered her tennis racquet and bag and stood to leave. Gil did the same as he continued his conversation with Bradley. "Sure. She's right here." He handed the telephone to Dani.

"Hi, Bradster! How was the party?" She and Gil proceeded to the car as Gil took her bag from her and carried it along with his. He listened to Dani laugh and watched the animation on her face as she talked to Bradley. "Yes, that is just what Jesus would have done too." She looked at Gil and laughed at something Brad said. "Not yet. I guess we're going to the football game tonight. . .okay. We'll be there to get you in just a few minutes. Me too. . .yes, I'll tell him. Bye, Brad." She handed the telephone back to Gil. "The man said to tell you he loves you." She contentedly swung her racquet and began humming a tune.

"It won't be long and he will be a man," Gil mused as they arrived at his car. "He's growing so fast I can hardly keep him in shoes or clothes!" He put their bags in the back and the two of them got into the vehicle. "What was it 'Jesus would have done too'?" he asked.

"I'll let Brad tell you. Well, get me home, driver! I've got to get cleaned up for my date with two handsome fellas tonight!"

After the football game later that evening Gil made hot cocoa for the three of them. Bradley was getting sleepy and went to get ready for bed. Gil made sure he brushed his teeth and then took him to his room. Brad yawned and returned his dad's hug.

"Could Dani come up and tuck me in, Daddy?" he asked.

"I suppose so," Gil said, surprised at his son's request. He went to the door and called down the stairs to Danielle, who came up the steps with a question on her face.

"He wants you to tuck him in," Gil said quietly with a shrug of his shoulders. He waited in the hallway, listening and watching. He saw Dani bend down to touch a kiss to Brad's forehead and brush his hair away from his eyes. The tenderness in her look and Brad's sleepy admiration for Dani brought an unexpected tear to Gil's eyes.

"Good night, Brad. Want to pray?"

"Will you, Dani? I'm so sleepy. . ."

"Sure, sweetheart. Dear Jesus, keep us safe tonight. Thank

You for the fun day each of us had today. Thank You for Daddy. Thank You for Grandma and Grandpa and Aunt Emily. Amen."

"And Rocky too, don't forget," Brad reminded her with another yawn.

"And Rocky too. Amen."

"Amen. Good night, Dani."

"Good night, Brad," she whispered.

Gil watched as she gently stroked his hair for a minute and noted that Brad was asleep before Dani rose from his bed. She smiled at Gil as she closed the door behind her. Gil placed his hands on either side of Dani's face and brought his lips down to hers. He felt her respond to his kiss as he pulled her into his embrace. He allowed his mouth to linger on hers before releasing her. Dani said nothing and they descended the stairs together. She started to walk toward the kitchen, but Gil took her hand and led her into the family room where he sat next to her on the sofa and untied the bow around her ponytail. He ran a hand through the soft silkiness of her hair and again embraced her, eager to feel her body against his and her lips on his. He touched his lips to hers once more and leaned back, cradling her in his embrace. Neither of them spoke for several seconds.

"Your tenderness with Brad made me want some for myself," he said finally. He again ran his fingers through her hair and noticed the way her eyelashes lay on her flushed cheeks. "You are so beautiful, Danielle. You're beautiful in a lot of ways. Here in my arms—and at the bedside of my son." He touched a kiss to her forehead and watched her mouth curve upward in a smile.

"Bradley makes people beautiful. He is so easy to love and love softens people—takes away the hard edges."

"There's nothing hard about you either, Dani. I think you would be easy to love too." He didn't give her time to respond, but drew her close for another kiss. He did not remember ever wanting Melinda like he suddenly—perhaps not so suddenly—wanted Danielle. He knew he wouldn't make excuses if she came on to him like Melinda did. But it didn't happen.

"I really need to go, Gil," she said. He released her and rose to his feet, extending his hand to her, which she took as she got up.

"I'm not scaring you away, am I?" he asked, brushing her hair back away from her face.

"No. *I'm* scaring me away," she admitted with a small, nervous laugh. She walked to the door and allowed him to help her on with her coat.

"Spend the day with us tomorrow?" he asked.

"Thanks, but I've made plans. Will I see you at church?" She pulled her keys from her pocket.

"I guess we'll try to make it. Brad does look forward to it. I'll walk you to your door. . ." He walked with her and they said their good nights at her front door.

Gil was pensive as he settled back in for the evening and turned on the television. He liked Dani. He was attracted to her physically, but it was more than that. He liked the way she treated Bradley. He liked the way she even talked to Brad on the telephone! She was animated and genuine with him. And he thought she liked him too. She responded to his kisses and seemed to enjoy being with him—even without Rocky being around. He could see that they could develop a deep relationship easily. He was ready to get serious with someone and Brad needed a mother. Dani might be the perfect woman for both of them.

At church that Sunday Gil saw little of Dani, but he made the acquaintance of a man who was the defensive line coach for the team they had just watched play the previous evening. He also met the families of some of Brad's friends. A skit that was done during the course of the service left him with questions, however, and he never recalled church making him so ill at ease —especially two weeks in a row. He decided he'd ask Dani some pointed questions the next time they got together, which he hoped would be soon. But as it turned out, it was some time before he or Brad saw Dani again.

Gil was back at work ten hours a day and Brad had developed some fast, close friendships at school and at the day care center. Gil began finding it easy to spend more time at work while Brad spent his long evenings at the homes of different friends. Finally on a late Thursday evening three weeks after his date with Dani, Gil made a point to call her. He got no answer, but just as he was about to leave a message, he saw Dani walking by the house with Rocky. He went to the front door to call to her.

"Getting kind of late for a stroll, isn't it?" he asked.

Dani beamed at him and came up the walk with Rocky beside her. "Yes, I guess it is. But the Rock needed the exercise. I was going to give you or Brad a call tonight. Is he still up?"

"I assume he is, but he's staying with a buddy tonight. I just got in a few minutes ago, obviously. Still in my monkey suit," he said, loosening his tie. "I haven't had supper yet. Want to go get a quick bite with me?"

"Sure. Let me take Rocky home."

Gil ran up the stairs and changed into a jogging suit and his running shoes before Dani came back. He met her at the door and they drove to a nearby restaurant. After they ordered, Gil took the liberty of reaching across the table to grasp Dani's hand.

"I've missed seeing you. Been working a lot?" he asked.

"No. I think you're the one who's been doing that," she

answered, dropping her eyes. She looked up quickly. "I hope that didn't sound catty."

He smiled, running a finger across the smooth surface of her hand. "No, it didn't, but you're right. All my big plans to cut back at work have quickly evaporated. It's been easy to let it happen now that Brad has become more established. He has his buddies to occupy his time." He expected her to say "He needs his dad's time," but she didn't. She simply nodded her head.

"I was going to call to check on Brad. You haven't had him to Sunday school for two weeks now." She wasn't smiling, but she didn't draw her hand away either. She looked concerned, but not angry.

"Yeah. I'm sorry about that. We've just been busy the past two weekends. Went to the folks' one weekend and then out of town to visit Lisa's parents last Sunday. Brad has missed it. He asked me already this week if we're going this Sunday." He released her hand as their waitress brought his food. Dani just sipped the hot chocolate she had ordered.

"Are you?" She held her mug between her hands.

"Planning on it. I have to confess, Dani, your church makes me a little uncomfortable sometimes. That skit a few weeks ago really threw me. In fact," he said between bites, "I don't think I understood it."

"What didn't you understand?"

Gil ate some more of his sandwich and fries before answering. He liked the way Dani seemed content to wait for him to speak. She never needed to "fill the air with words" to make him feel at ease or, apparently, to put herself at ease. The tension of the week evaporated as he sat with her. He looked into the clear blue of her expressive eyes and told her so.

"I've missed seeing you, Dani. I like spending time with you. I like having you spend time with Brad and me. You help me keep things in perspective." He regarded her intently for a few seconds before going on. "Anyway, to answer your question, at the end of that skit the implication was that the guy—who had done a lot of good things in his life—wasn't going to go to heaven. It was also suggested that the woman, who didn't have any 'good deeds,' for lack of a better term, *did* go to heaven. Did I understand that correctly?"

"Yes, you did. Gil, let me ask you a question." She set her cup back down. "What do you think you need to 'do' to go to heaven when you die?"

"I guess I'd have to say that I'd have to do a lot more good things than bad things. Is that right?" he asked, partly serious, partly baiting her.

"Not exactly," she replied with a small smile.

Gil chuckled slightly. "Somehow I *knew* you were going to say that." He became pensive again. "Brad speaks of going to heaven to see his mother. Before he was in your Sunday school class, he never said anything about heaven. Maybe he knew I wouldn't have an answer to any question he might ask in that regard."

"So let's return to my first question. What do you—or does anyone—need to do to go to heaven when this life is over? That was the question left hanging in the air by that skit at church."

Gil thought again, slowly nibbling at his food. "Like I said," he finally replied, "I do think it has something to do with do-ing good things and not wrong things. Like teaching Sunday school and not stealing from someone."

"There was a time I thought that way too," she said. "But then someone shared the facts about the gospel of Jesus Christ with me. First she told me that heaven wasn't something I could hope to merit, but that it's a gift. The only 'good thing' God requires is belief in His Son, Jesus Christ. In fact, in the

Gospel of John in the New Testament, some people asked Jesus, 'What must we do to do the works of God?' Jesus' response was both simple and surprising. He said, 'The work of God is to believe in the one he has sent.' "

"Anything else?" the waitress asked, coming up to their table.

"No, thanks. Just the bill," Gil reached for his wallet and their conversation ceased as they made their way to the cash register and then the car. Once they were in the car and on their way home, Gil thought about what Dani had said. She seemed content during the short trip to let him think about what she had told him.

"I'd like to talk some more about this," he said as he pulled into his driveway. "Can you come in for a while?"

"Why don't you come to my place? Mom made some great cookies this morning."

Gil agreed and they walked to Dani's. They talked with her parents for a few minutes before going to the living room by themselves, away from the television. Gil noted with some chagrin that Rocky fell into step behind them.

Great, he thought. *The canine baby-sitter.*

As Gil sat on the sofa beside Dani, Rocky placed himself squarely in front of them, his large head resting warily on his front paws. As usual, he watched Gil with almost tangible hostility. Or so Gil thought. Absence hadn't made Rocky's heart grow any fonder towards him. That was obvious. Gil shook his head clear of thoughts about Rocky.

"That stuff about believing in Jesus sounds too easy, Dani. Way too easy. There's got to be a catch."

"There is and there isn't," she answered, stroking Rocky's head. "Belief or trust is simple enough for a child to exercise— like Brad. But for us who are used to doing it our own way, belief in someone else to the extent Jesus calls for is not easy. It calls for us to recognize that there is no way we can please God enough to measure up to His perfect standard. So we have to admit to that—to being sinners. We have to be genuinely sorry for our sin by seeing it with God's eyes. And then we have to turn from it, which proves that we agree with what God says about sin. That's what repentance is and what Jesus said was needed to enter heaven upon death."

"So then. . . ?" he asked.

"Once you agree with God that you're a sinner, you ask for His forgiveness and commit your life to Him. He becomes not only your Savior, but your Master as well. The place for good deeds then is not to earn heaven, but to please the One who gave it to you as a gift. Obedience follows the receiving of what Jesus called the abundant life."

"I've never heard anything like that before," Gil admitted.

"That was the point of the skit at church. A person cannot hope to earn or merit heaven based on what he has or hasn't done. Are you familiar with the account of Jesus' death on the cross?" she asked.

"Yes. I've been a regular Easter and Christmas churchgoer," Gil confessed with a smile.

"Then you know that the thieves who died next to Jesus had no time to do anything good. Their time had run out. One simply said to Jesus, 'Remember me when you come into your kingdom.' And Jesus told him: 'Today you will be with me in paradise.' For that man, for the woman in that skit at church, for any of us, the only way to heaven is to receive it as a gift from the God who offers it through His Son."

"I see," he said reflectively. He was thoughtful for the space of several seconds. "So how does someone receive this gift?"

"By praying in faith and asking God for it. I can pray with you right now and you can ask Jesus Christ to become the Lord of your life."

"Just like that? Pray a prayer and boom! I'm in heaven?" he asked. Suddenly he was very skeptical.

"Like I said, it's not that easy. It's simple, it's straightforward, but it's not easy. Committing your life to Jesus Christ is a step of faith. And even the faith comes from God," she said. "But God gives it just as generously as He gives life in His Son, Jesus Christ."

Gil returned her own intent look and thought about her words. It all made sense. But there was something else that was nagging at the back of his consciousness. He couldn't put his finger on it, but he knew he wasn't ready to pray and "make everything better" either.

"I need to think about this, Dani," he said. "But thanks for telling me all this. I've never understood a lot about Jesus and all that. This believing and praying. . .this is what Bradley did, isn't it?"

"Yes," she said, smiling at the memory. "And your sister Emily did some time ago. It's what we all must do if we want to spend our forever with God. There is no other way." Gil reached to touch the softness of her face, locking in his memory the gentle intensity of her look. He saw more in her eyes than he could explain. It almost pained him and he didn't know why. He dropped his hand and his gaze.

"How about those cookies?" he asked, the moment gone.

"Sure," she said and got up to go to the kitchen. Gil looked at Rocky who stared back at him in stony silence.

"So who asked you?" Gil asked. He received a narrow-eyed look in return as Rocky's upper lip curled back slightly, exposing his upper teeth.

"The feeling's mutual, buddy," he said. *I can't believe it!* he said to himself. *I'm talking to a dog!* He regarded Rocky for a few more seconds and thought he would make one more attempt at gaining the dog's esteem. He snapped his fingers.

"Come here, Rock. Let's try to bury the hatchet. What do you say?" He held his hand out, his palm up and open. Rocky didn't move, but Gil saw his tail swish back and forth once or twice. He tried again. "I'm willing to meet you halfway for the sake of your mistress," Gil said. "I plan to kiss her again tonight and I want to leave here in one unbloodied piece, thank you very much." Rocky still sat, his gaze unyielding and his paws unmoving. But his tail wagged a little more. Gil figured that was a sign of his weakening.

"Come on, old boy. You like your mistress. You like my son. Why not make the effort to like me? God knows. . ." He hesitated when he heard himself say that. He continued again. "God knows I'm trying my best to like you." He couldn't believe it when Rocky rose to his feet and came over and nuzzled his hand with his cool, wet nose. Gil scratched Rocky's ears and let his hand run down the length of the dog's back. "Now, that's not so bad, is it?" *I'm talking to a dog. All this talk about God and being with Dani is making me nuts.*

"Don't tell me you two are going to try to come to an understanding!" Dani walked back into the room carrying a tray with two glasses of milk and a plate of cookies. Rocky abruptly turned from Gil and went over to Dani.

"We're trying," Gil said, taking the tray from her and setting it down on the coffee table. "If I ever plan to kiss you again without leaving part of my anatomy in Rocky's mouth, I thought I'd better make the first attempt at friendship—or peaceful coexistence at least." He sampled one of the cookies as Dani sat back down beside him and Rocky resumed his place on the floor in front of them. "Hey! These are great!" Gil concurred. "Now I know where you learned your culinary skills!"

The rest of their evening was relaxing and enjoyable for Gil.

They had moments of laughter and times of seriousness. Times of playfulness and times of tenderness. The ever-watchful Rocky never left the room, but he no longer raised a menacing glare to Gil. He seemed to be watching and evaluating the situation and Gil himself. There were minutes when Gil forgot he was even in the room. But Gil never forgot the earlier discussion he had with Dani. It kept coming back to him long after he left her house and finally lay in his bed, unable to sleep.

By two in the morning, he was still tossing fitfully. He got out of bed and went to his window. He looked over to Dani's house and saw an upstairs light on. He wondered if she were still awake too. He paced the room and ran his hand through his bed-rumpled hair. What was bothering him? What undefined something was nagging at him? Suddenly, he knew what it was. His pacing stopped.

It was Lisa. Lisa and God. One of the last things Lisa had said to him about God before she died.

"I have peace, Gil," she had said in a barely audible voice. "I've talked with God and I know all will be right for me and for you and Brad too. I know it." Gil had wanted to scream at her and at God.

PEACE? How could he have peace? He wanted his wife! How could God take his young wife and leave him and their son to go on without her? Was this some kind of joke? He had wanted to say to Lisa: That's great, Lisa. But I don't have any peace. None! Brad and I are in the real world! We're going to be stuck here without you while you and your God bask away in the sun somewhere!

But he hadn't said anything. He had just nodded his head, held her hand, and wondered why this was happening to them. And he had never prayed again—not for Lisa to get better, not for God to help him with Brad, not for anything. His anger had dissipated in the face of cool indifference. He had envied Lisa her peace in a way, but it brought none to him. So he had just gone on with Brad. Just the two of them getting from one day to the next until life settled into a pattern. There was no contentment or peace for him, but he figured it wasn't obtainable anyway. It was for old people. Sick people. People who were dying. . .like Lisa, not like him.

"Angry," he said aloud. "I was angry with You, God. I'm still angry with You. No," he mused, "no, it's not anger. Indifference. I've just been indifferent to You. For years. Lisa needed You for peace. I just needed time. I made it on my own, no thanks to You, I thought. But my anger didn't go away with time, did it? It just changed form. I was simply indifferent to You or anything that had to do with You. And the peace. . .well, the peace wasn't there for the taking. And I, for sure, wasn't there for the asking."

Time had brought resolution, but never peace. He had pushed it away. He had pushed God away. But God had pushed His way back into his life—in Emily, in Brad, and now in Dani. And Gil had a feeling God wouldn't be pushed away anymore. He, Gil Stewart, would have to make a decision. Somehow he had come to a turning point. He thought back over the evening he had spent with Danielle. The moment he had touched her face was the point of confrontation. He had seen it then.

Longing. Compassion. Not Dani's. It was in Dani, yet it was beyond her at the same time. It was God's compassion for *him*. God's longing for him. God's love for him. God's. . .peace for him. He and Dani had talked of heaven and eternal life. But he connected heaven with peace and peace with God. . .and neither with himself. He had detached himself from both. He had his son. He had his work. He had his sporting interests. But he had no peace, no settled feeling of contentment or fulfillment.

He was indifferent to it all, or so he thought. But that skit, weeks ago, had started him thinking. He couldn't continue living with this deeply buried indifference. He couldn't explain it, wasn't sure he understood it, but he sensed God was calling to him, reaching out to him. He would do what Dani said.

Gil went to his knees beside his bed and began to pray. He prayed for hours.

By the next morning Gil Stewart had a new life. Gil Stewart had eternal life. The indifference, the skepticism that he had kept just under the surface for so many years, was gone. He had peace with the God who made him. He had been born of the Spirit of God. He had been born again. When he awoke in the morning, he called his sister.

"Hi, Em. Wasn't sure I'd catch you home."

"You almost didn't. I was just on my way out the door. What's on your mind?"

Suddenly Gil felt a little nervous. How would he say this? *No way to do it, but just say it.* "I wanted to tell you that I had quite a talk with Danielle last night," he began.

"And. . . ? You're getting married?"

"Not that I know of," he said. "But, you know, that doesn't sound like a bad idea. I'll give it some thought." He paused and took a deep breath. "No, what I called to tell you was that. . .uh . . .I'm not sure how I say this, but I prayed to God last night and—"

"And you got saved?" Her voice was a squeal. He could see her expression by the tone of her voice.

"If that means I was born again, yes."

"Oh, Gil! I am so thrilled! I've been praying for you for so long! Tell me all about it!"

"I thought you had some place to go. . . ?"

"It can wait. I'm sitting down right now and you tell me everything!"

After Gil had told her about his conversation with Danielle, his sleepless night, and finally his time of praying, she was as excited as he had ever heard her.

"Now you be sure to go and tell Dani! And tell Brad as soon as he comes home! I think I'm going to have to come for a visit this weekend to give you a big hug and a 'welcome to the family of God' kiss. I love you, big brother! Thanks for calling me. You have made my day!" They talked a few more minutes and Gil went to get the morning paper.

Dani was just coming out her door, dressed in her running attire, Rocky at her side. She waved to Gil and walked over.

"Want to take a run with us?" she asked. Rocky looked as friendly as he ever had. Well, not *friendly*, but less guarded than Gil had ever seen him. He looked eager for a run.

"Yes, I think I would. Come on in while I change. You can bring the Rock in," he said, holding the door open for both of them.

He ran upstairs, grabbed his socks, shoes, and sunglasses, and quickly came back down the steps. He sat down in the chair to put on his socks and shoes. Dani stood near the door while Rocky sniffed around the entryway carpet.

"Were you up late last night?" Gil asked, tying his shoes. "I was and saw a light on."

"Yes," she answered simply. "Couldn't you sleep?"

Gil stood up and reached for his sunglasses. "No. I was busy. Praying."

Dani's eyes widened. "Praying. . . ?"

"Yeah, I. . ." He scratched the back of his neck and gave her a sheepish grin. "I thought a lot about what we had talked about earlier last night. And, well, I'm not sure I did it right, but I just asked God to give me the gift you talked about. I admitted my sin to Him—once I got to thinking about it, it was more than I had thought! And I just, well, I just prayed for a long time and told Him that, for what it was worth, I wanted to go His way the rest of my life."

Gil was surprised as Dani's eyes filled with tears. He had expected a reaction like Emily's—not this!

"Hey! I wasn't trying to get your day off to a bad start!" He reached for a box of tissues and offered them to her. She took one and dabbed at her eyes. She bit down lightly on her lower lip. Rocky looked up at her questioningly.

"It's okay, Rock," Gil quickly assured him. "I didn't hurt your 'mom.' "

Dani laughed and dropped Rocky's leash. She wiped at her eyes again and then her nose. She surprised Gil by stepping up to him and bringing her lips up to his for a kiss.

"You can't know how happy this makes me," she said, cupping his face in her hands. "I was up praying for you most of the night."

"For what?" he asked.

"For just what happened. For you to surrender yourself to Jesus." She stepped back from him again and wiped away the still-gathering tears. "We've got to tell Brad," she said emphatically, but with a gentle smile.

"We will when he gets home. But first, tell me again how happy I've made you," he said, drawing her back into his arms for a long kiss.

A car horn sounded and they looked up to see Brad coming up the walk. Rocky gave a loud bark and his tail began an eager wagging from side to side. Brad broke into a run for the door.

"Rocky!" he exclaimed, reaching for the dog. He looked up at Dani and his father. "Hi, Dad! Hi, Dani!" he said. "You guys going running?"

"Yeah. Let's grab your bike and you can go with us," Gil said, ruffling his son's hair.

"Great! It'll be the four of us again!"

Gil looked at Dani as she lovingly smiled at Brad, kneeling down to hug him. He knew it would be the four of them for a long time to come. *Thank You, God,* he thought as he went to get Bradley's bicycle.

CHAPTER 7

Gennao

Jesus declared, ". . .no one can see the kingdom of God
unless he is [gennao] born again."
—John 3:3 NIV

Jenna angrily wiped the unwanted tears from her face and regarded her twin sister with a challenge in her eyes.

"So what are you trying to tell me, Janet? If I drop Brian like Ron dumped me, life will be just lovely?" she asked with undisguised sarcasm.

Janet shifted her weight in her chair and set her mug of coffee down. She met Jenna's hard but hurting look with a tranquil tenderness that took more fight out of Jenna, though she would never admit it to herself, let alone to her sister.

"What I'm trying to say, Jen, is that maybe now you're starting to realize that any lasting contentment in life isn't going to come from Brian or Ron or anyone else. Even if you and Brian get married tomorrow, there are things Brian can never be for you. Things he can never do for you. There are things you can never do for yourself."

"Are you going to get preachy on me, Jan?" Jenna asked. "That's Matt's job," she said. Her twin's husband, Matthew, was pastor of a small church.

"We've talked about your need of Jesus Christ before," Janet replied quietly.

"No," Jenna countered. "*You've* talked about my 'need of Jesus Christ before.' "

Janet was not going to quibble about details. "All right," she agreed, "*I've* talked about your need to surrender the control of your life to Jesus Christ before. But hear me out." Janet hesitated and prayed quickly. *At least she hasn't already bolted out the door, Lord!* She went on, slowly and gently.

"You've always been the headstrong one of the two of us, Jenna. You've always gone after what you wanted with a passion that amazes me. But Jesus Christ did not give you life for you to please Jenna Randall. He gave you life so that you could please and serve Him. Tell me, Jen, just what in your life to this point has pleased or served the Lord who made you in any way?"

Janet could see that a quick retort came to Jenna's mind, but waited quietly as Jenna pensively considered her question. Jenna's acerbic response vanished as quickly as it had come. The empty look in her troubled blue eyes spoke volumes to Janet. Defeat. Doubt. Perhaps despair.

"Nothing," she said simply and honestly. "Absolutely nothing."

Jenna mutely waved the last of her soggy tissues. Taking her cue, Janet went down the hallway for a fresh supply.

Jenna's realization of what she had admitted to her sister and to herself brought her to a dead end. Her future, which should be giving her reason to be happy, instead was giving her restless nights and self-doubts. Her past? She had been playing her way through life like a game. Now, for reasons she could not understand, she felt like she was going to lose at this game she thought she had played so well. And the irony of it all was that it wasn't a game. It had never been a game.

Janet returned with a box of tissues and squeezed into the chair beside her twin to comfort her, just as she had done when they were children. She gave Jenna's shoulder a gentle hug. Jenna looked at her sister again with vacant eyes. How was it that she, Jenna Kathryn Randall, sitting in a worn chair in her sister's apartment, was making a confession that she would have scorned only months ago? Jenna wasn't scoffing now.

What had brought her to this impasse? She closed her eyes and remembered. . . .

Jenna discreetly raised her hand to her mouth to cover a yawn she could no longer suppress. She looked at her watch and was surprised to find it was only ten-thirty. Her boyfriend, Ron, caught her eyes from across the crowded room where he was engaged in a lively discussion with some other men over the day's collegiate football games. He gave her a wink, but quickly turned back to his discussion. Jenna found an available seat on the closest chair and sat down, wishing they could exit the party and she could just go home to bed.

"Jenna, can I get you some more to drink?" Their host, a boyishly handsome man whose curly black hair and runner's lean build belied his thirty-four years, came up beside her. Jenna gave her ash-blond hair a brush away from her face and set her empty glass down on the end table. She absently fingered the string of pearls at her neck and smiled with more energy than she felt.

"No, thanks, Garth." She returned a wave to someone across the room who had just entered, although Garth didn't look up. She turned her attention back to him. Garth was quietly appraising her and Jenna gave her host a beguiling smile.

"Just what are you thinking?" she asked.

Garth chuckled and ran a finger gently down the length of her arm to her fingertips. He took another sip of his own beverage and gave her a baiting look. "Maybe we should get together for old time's sake, Jen. Just a fun night. The two of us."

"You've had too much to drink, Garth. We're old history," she said, covering another yawn. "Besides, you're getting married next month. Remember?"

"Well, married isn't dead and I'm neither yet. Since when did 'married' make a difference to you anyway?" His smile was an aloof, calculated one.

"That too is old history and none of your business," she retorted with no pretense of a smile now.

"It was my business at the time, Jenna," he said quietly. There was no smile—aloof or otherwise—on Garth's face now either. "The guy was almost twice your age and had two kids. And you left me for him! I don't get it, Jen. I don't get it now and I didn't get it then!"

Jenna rose to her feet, her face flushed with irritation. "That's enough, Garth," she bristled, her voice just above a whisper.

"Honey, could you come and give me a hand a minute?"

Garth's fiancée came up to them, oblivious to what had just transpired. She turned to Jenna.

"Hi, Jen. Sorry I haven't had much time to talk with you. Enjoying yourself?" she asked.

I was, Jenna thought, but she pasted on a smile. "Sure! Nice party, Christina."

"Meet me in the kitchen, Garth. I need to catch Colleen before she gets away." Christina walked away, leaving Jenna alone again with Garth. He looked somewhat contrite.

"Sorry, Jen. I was out of line. You look good tonight—brings back memories." He raised his glass to her and walked away.

"See you," is what Jenna said as she went to get Ron. *Grow up, Garth,* was what she thought. *You're not the one to be dragging skeletons out of my closet.*

After the party and after dismissing Ron because she felt ill, Jenna sank into the inviting warmth of her waterbed. Sleep eluded her, however, as she mulled over Garth's earlier comments.

Jenna had been living with Garth when she met Brian. She didn't think she had ever loved anyone like she loved Brian—not even Ron, her current boyfriend. Brian was ruggedly handsome, mature, intelligent, attentive, and rich. His job as an airline pilot meant he was away from home a lot. Even though they both lived in the Chicago area, they had met at a hotel in Atlanta. He had told her from the beginning that he was married. Jenna's modern attitude was that if a woman couldn't keep her man, that was her problem. Any man with enough good qualities was fair game as far as she was concerned. And Brian had more than his share of good qualities.

Soon after meeting Brian, Jenna broke off her relationship with Garth and moved into a condo in Lombard. For a year Brian showered her with extravagant gifts and special weekend getaways. He made her feel recklessly wonderful and pampered. But month after month he remained married, declaring he would leave his wife the next month or after the holiday or after. . .something. After thirteen months, Jenna had given him an ultimatum: Divorce her or it's over. He had laughed off her ultimatum.

"Give me time, Jay," he had said. "Caroline can be vicious," he said. He had to bide his time and make sure Caroline didn't clean him out financially.

So Jenna had given him time and time, and more time. Until the day she saw Caroline and their children. Brian's wife was not the homely shrew Brian had said she was. She was a beautiful woman with kind, laughing eyes, and had an obvious joyful love for her children. Jenna had seen her getting into Brian's car at the grocery store one day. The luxury sports car with the FLYBOY license plate left no doubt as to Caroline's identity.

So that was Caroline: "prudish, overweight, whiney Caroline." Jenna had cried the rest of the day. She walked away from Brian's empty promises and his teasing blue eyes. She sent a note to him through the airline that she would not see him anymore. If he tried to see her, she would go to Caroline and tell her everything.

He sent flowers. She threw them in the trash. He left messages she didn't return. He sent notes or letters she didn't read. She was through with Brian. She wouldn't be taken in by his love talk or lovemaking anymore. But suddenly one evening, he had shown up at her door.

"We need to talk," he said.

By the time he had left, the only talk had been Brian's promises of leaving Caroline and marrying Jenna. Jenna could not resist his pleas, and their passion left little room for argument. But he had not come back again. No cards, no calls, no gifts. It was like she had imagined their last night together. Her pride kept her from calling him and her shame kept her from calling his wife.

That had been two years ago. Now, Jenna had begun to feel she was really starting over. She and Ron had been seeing each other for a few months. Ron was special and unattached. Brian was old history, just like she told Garth. But Garth bringing up Brian again left her feeling uneasy. She punched her pillow and told herself to let it all go and get to sleep. Yet her disquieting thoughts were still at the edge of her consciousness when she finally slept.

The next day, Jenna was sicker than she had ever been in all her twenty-six years. She couldn't keep any food down; just the smell of making tea sent her running to the bathroom for another ten minutes of retching and vomiting. She didn't think she had a fever; she decided it must be food poisoning. She looked at her clock. It was only seven! She lie back down, and was awakened a few hours later by the telephone. She answered in a groggy voice, afraid moving would start the room spinning.

"Feeling a little rough this afternoon, are we?" Ron asked in a teasing voice. "Too much partying last night?"

" 'Little rough' is hardly an apt description. Are you okay? I think I must have gotten food poisoning! Maybe one of those mushrooms was a toadstool!" Jenna sat up slowly on the corner of her bed.

"I didn't eat mushrooms, so maybe. Can I get you something at the pharmacy?" he asked.

"Please. I'm going to try and take a shower, so just leave it outside my door if I don't answer."

"Will do. If I don't see you, I'll call you later, babe."

After Jenna took a shower, she did feel better. She found a package from the pharmacy outside her door, so she missed Ron. After reading a little of the current novel she'd been working her way through for a week, she felt better and had some toast and tea. By five o'clock she felt fine and put on her jeans and a plaid shirt to make a trip to get some groceries, including crackers in case she had a relapse. Her doorbell rang just as she was about to leave. She opened the door to face a handsome man with an armful of red roses. Jenna's heart lurched.

"Brian!"

She couldn't believe it was him. He raised his sunglasses and looked at her intently with his ice-blue eyes. His hair had grayed slightly at the temples, but he looked every bit as wonderful as she remembered him. He looked better than she remembered him. He held out the roses and Jenna held onto the door for support.

"I had to see you, Jay. May I come in? Just to talk?" Jenna hesitated and he put his free hand against the door. "Please. I won't stay if you don't want me to."

Dozens of images flashed through Jenna's mind and dozens of feelings coursed through her as well. Talk was one thing they didn't do much of the last time Brian had come to her condo, claiming that was what he wanted then. She thought of that last night and the promises that never materialized. *Well,* she thought, *two can play this game. I'll let him speak his piece and then throw him out. Let him beg. I'd like nothing better.*

"A few minutes," she said without emotion, opening the door wider.

"Got a vase for these?" he asked.

She went to the kitchen and returned with a vase filled with water. She took the flowers from him and wordlessly arranged them in the vase and set them on the piano. Brian came up behind her, gently grasping her arms. She steeled herself against his touch and stepped away from him. She sat down in her favorite chair, motioning for him to have a seat on the couch. She readied herself for what she was sure would be a well-rehearsed speech.

"What's the occasion?" she asked. "Did you finally get divorced or do you need to wait until after the Bears' game?"

He laughed and loosened his tie, leaning back easily on the sofa as if he'd just come home from a long flight. "It's my birthday, Jay, remember?" Jay. His nickname for her. His eyes never left her face and his cool aloofness began to make Jenna both uneasy and angry.

"You're. . .forty-six now, aren't you?"

I should have never let him in. The room was filled with Brian's cologne and Brian's confident air. His gentle tone at the door had been left there. Jenna was again facing Brian as she knew him: charming, relaxed, self-assured to the point of arrogance, and in charge. She shifted in her chair.

"Yeah," he answered easily. "I still lift a few times a week and play tennis regularly. You're looking great, Jay. I like the way you've got your hair fixed. Hey. . .got anything to drink?"

She got up to get away from his surreptitious smile and went to the kitchen again.

"The diet stuff with a lot of ice. You know how I like it," he called.

From the time Jenna brought the soda to Brian to when he left early the next morning, the evening was a replay of his last visit. She had neither "made him beg" nor thrown him out. His words of love, his whispered promises, and his tender kisses had disarmed her. She willingly gave herself to him, just as she had so many times before. She felt used, but at the same time, victorious. Brian still loved her! It was her he came back to and no one else! His passion and promises brought her love for him up from some hidden place in her heart. He repeatedly said he was sorry he had "stepped away" for so long. He said he not only wanted her, he needed her—more than anything or anyone.

"I've missed you so, Jay," he kept saying. "We can't let go of what we had." And she had succumbed to his words and his touch and the entreaty in his eyes. She had missed him too; she didn't realize just how much until he was back in her arms again.

After Brian left the next morning, however, she was troubled. It was so easy to pick up where they had left off—too easy. She berated herself in hindsight for giving in to him so readily. Maybe her constant tiredness lately left her with less than her usual strong-willed constitution. She sipped her morning coffee and smiled pathetically. Who was she kidding? She never had a strong constitution when it came to Brian.

"I guess it's true after all," she said aloud. "Absence does make the heart. . ." A wave of nausea overcame her and she put down the coffee quickly, eager to get away from even the smell of it. "What is this?"

She sat down on the couch and took some deep breaths. As she did, she faced the calendar on her kitchen wall and her heart skipped a beat. Her menstrual period, always on time, was late. It was very late. She looked frantically back at the days, trying to remember when she had had her birth control pill prescription changed. She and Ron had been careful during the changeover, but the fact was there. She hadn't been through her cycle in over two months. *NO!* she screamed inwardly. *I can't be!* She kept trying to put dates, pills, and "events" together, but her mind wouldn't work. The next thing she knew, she was in her bathroom again, as sick as she had been the previous morning.

Afterwards, she returned to her kitchen and called off sick from work. Then she grabbed the telephone book and anxiously looked under "Birth Control" in the yellow pages. A girl at work had mentioned a place that offered free pregnancy tests. Jenna's trembling hand went down the page until she found the Crisis Pregnancy Center. *If I am pregnant,* she thought, *it would certainly qualify as a crisis.* She made the call and an appointment. Her doorbell rang as soon as she finished her call. *Please, don't let it be Brian. . .* She made sure the chain lock was in place before opening the door.

"Hey, babe! You okay? I called your office and they said you had called in sick. You're still not better?" Ron stood there, his mirror sunglasses hiding his warm brown eyes. Jenna thought she probably didn't look very good; she assuredly didn't feel very good.

"Ron. . .no, I'm still under the weather," she said weakly. She brushed her hair out of her eyes and took a long, slow, deep breath.

"Aren't you going to invite me in?" he asked. "Or are you lethally contagious?"

Jenna unlatched the door and motioned him in with a mumbled apology. "I'm sorry. I'm forgetting my manners."

Ron threw his sunglasses and light jacket on the chair. He pointed casually at the piano. "Nice flowers! From anyone I know?"

Jenna had forgotten all about the roses. She glanced around quickly to make sure Brian hadn't left anything. Sitting down on the sofa, she took a drink of water to gain a few extra seconds to think. "Yeah. My dad—just to say 'hi,' he said," she lied.

"Sounds like something your old man would do," he replied offhandedly. "So, you're looking pale, babe. Have you been sick since I last talked to you?" He sat down across from her, rubbing his hand across his closely shaven beard.

"Yes," she lied again. "That's why I didn't answer your call last night. I just wasn't feeling well." She wondered if she should tell him about her missed cycles. She had no idea how he would react.

"Maybe you should call a doctor and make sure it's nothing serious. Usually the flu is here and gone in twenty-four hours." He looked at his watch and stood. "I have to go out of town for the rest of the week, so I'm going to run home, change clothes, and catch a late flight to D.C. I'll call to check on you, babe.

Let's plan a nice dinner out for Friday, okay? That gives you four more days to get better. I can find my way out," he said casually. "Take care of yourself, Jen." He blew her a kiss and was gone.

After Ron left, Jenna sat, holding her right lower abdomen, which had also been bothering her lately. She had forgotten about the occasional, nagging pain she had been having off and on for the past week or so. She had assumed she was ovulating. Now she didn't know what it meant, if anything. Was it something that went along with. . .pregnancy? She hoped not! She looked at the clock and decided to take a nap until it was time for her appointment.

Jenna sat nervously across from the woman at the pregnancy center. Her mouth was dry and she could feel the beginnings of a headache at her temples. After introductions, the woman named Barb explained to Jenna how to do her pregnancy test. Jenna allowed her to talk her through the procedure and wordlessly did as she was instructed.

"The test results will take about five minutes, Jenna," Barb explained. "Please sit down again. I need to ask you a few more questions."

After the expected questions about her address and telephone number and such, the more personal questions increased Jenna's tension.

"What are your intentions if you are pregnant?" Barb asked without rancor.

"I have no idea," Jenna answered truthfully.

"Does the father of the baby know you might be pregnant?"

"No."

"What would his reaction be if you are pregnant?"

Jenna hesitated. She and Ron had never talked about anything like this. And now that Brian was back in her life. . .Brian.

She was pretty sure what *his* reaction would be. "I. . .I don't know," she replied. "He's just started a new job and we have never discussed. . .anything like this."

"Do you have any church affiliation, Jenna?"

"No. I just went to church as a little kid."

"Are you on any medication or under any emotional stress? Anything that might effect your menstrual cycle?" Barb asked.

"Just birth control pills. My emotional stress is more recent— like today." *Like starting when Brian showed up yesterday,* she thought to herself.

"What are your feelings on abortion?" Barb asked, pausing in her writing.

"It's a way out of a tough situation." *And I'm in a tough situation.* Jenna was sure abortion was the only way out for her if she did end up pregnant.

"Let's check your test," Barb said. They stood together and Jenna looked at the test slide. A bold plus sign on the test slide sent her heart to her feet.

"I'm pregnant," she whispered.

"This only means you have a positive test, Jenna. A physician must make a diagnosis of pregnancy." Barb seemed to sense Jenna's numbing dismay and offered for her to sit down again. "A doctor needs to give you a blood test and an exam to confirm a pregnancy, Jenna. Do you have a regular physician?" she asked gently. Jenna nodded her head dumbly.

Pregnant! How did I get myself into this mess? What am I going to do? What will I tell Ron? What about Brian? These and a dozen other questions stormed through her throbbing head.

"We're here to help and support you in any way we can, Jenna. May I follow up with you by phone in a few days to see how you are?"

"Sure," Jenna answered, distracted by her own thoughts. *I*

can't afford an abortion! What if Brian finds out? What if Ron finds out about Brian? I've got to get out of here so I can think!

"Before you go, Jenna, I want to tell you something. I was once in your situation: facing the possibility of pregnancy and single parenthood. My boyfriend didn't want anything to do with a baby. We were both in college. I had no job, no health insurance, and then. . .no boyfriend either." Jenna looked at Barb, who was focused on her with empathy and gentleness. "So," she continued, "I got an abortion. I want you to know, Jenna, that was the most costly, wrong decision I ever made. For years I had terrible guilt and knew I could not undo what I had done." She smiled sympathetically at Jenna, who had forgotten her own despair for the moment.

"But a friend shared with me how Jesus Christ could help me and would forgive me—and help me forgive myself. Consider carefully what you do if you are pregnant, Jenna, because it will affect you for the rest of your life. The Lord Jesus Christ will not make all your problems disappear in a night, but—"

"I don't think even Jesus Christ could get me out of this mess," Jenna interrupted. "Thanks anyway." She reached for her purse.

"May I pray with you before you go?" Barb asked.

Jenna was caught off-guard. She thought people just prayed in church or at meals, like her holier-than-thou sister or brother-in-law. Or that a person had to be a priest or preacher or something to pray.

"May I?" Barb gently persisted.

"Sure," Jenna acquiesced. "I can use all the help I can get." She did not bow her head or close her eyes, but watched Barb do both.

"Dear Lord," Barb prayed, "You know all that Jenna is facing in her life right now. I pray that You will show her Your love for her and that You will give her guidance. If she is pregnant, help her to make the right decision for her baby and herself. I pray that she will truly seek You, Lord, and that You will bring her to Yourself. Amen." Barb looked up and touched Jenna's hand. "I'll keep praying for you, Jenna," she said, "and give you a call in a week or so. Let me give you some literature to read over, and I'll give you a form for your doctor that verifies your positive urine pregnancy test."

"Thank you for your prayer," Jenna said sincerely. She felt humbled, confused, and scared. She needed to get home and think.

"You're welcome. Thank you for allowing me to pray with you. I know it can be awkward, especially with a stranger." After she gave Jenna the information she had mentioned, Barb saw Jenna to the door, again telling her she would be in touch. Jenna left the building with tears beginning to sting her eyes.

When she walked into her condo, the telephone was ringing.

"Jay! Did I catch you at a bad time? I tried your number at work and they said you'd called in sick."

"I was sick. But I'm better now." She ran her hand across her abdomen. "I really didn't think I'd hear from you again so soon," she said, not wanting to talk to anyone at the moment.

"Well, listen, I'm on my way out of town, but I wanted to call you." He lowered his voice. "Last night was great, Jay. I want to see you again Friday. I need to see you again."

"I. . .can't, Brian. I've already got plans," she said, wishing her head would stop pounding.

"Break them. This is you and me, Jay. What is more important?"

If only you knew, she thought. "Something's come up, Brian, and I need to—"

"I need you, Jay. Just be there Friday night. I'll be out of town for three weeks starting Saturday. After these last two years, three weeks is too long. I've got to go. Love you," he said and hung up. Her protest was cut off midsentence by the drone of the broken connection. Knowing she had already made plans with Ron for Friday, she promised herself she'd sort it all out later. Jenna reached for her personal telephone book to call her physician. She tried not to think about how she would tell Ron she was pregnant when he called to check on her.

"You're WHAT?" Ron almost shouted into the telephone. Jenna held the receiver in her trembling hand. Another tear—she'd been crying all day—found its way down her cheek. She couldn't answer him.

"You're kidding, right, Jen?" he asked in a more controlled tone.

"Well, I haven't had a blood test yet, but the accuracy of these urine tests is greater than 95 percent," she said, repeating what Barb had told her. There was silence for several long seconds before Ron spoke again.

"Listen, Jenna, you know how I feel about you, but a baby just isn't in my game plan right now. If you need me to do it, I'll pay for an abortion."

"I don't know if I can do that, Ron. I mean, this is. . .this is a *baby*. Our baby." Jenna wished she hadn't looked at the pamphlets on human growth and development she had been given. None of the pictures of babies in early weeks of gestation looked like anything other than just that—babies.

"Baby? Jenna, get a hold of yourself! You can't be much more than a few weeks along. It's hardly a 'baby' yet!"

"But in the pictures the woman gave me at the—"

"Get rid of them. She's just some bleeding-heart Bible-thumper trying to put you on a guilt trip! Those people don't live in the real world." He hesitated briefly and went on, back in control again. "Listen, babe. I'll support you in and through this, but this isn't a good time for me. I'm not going to run out on you, but we simply can't try this parent thing now. The company may move me to California and I've still got some hefty school debts to pay off. Why don't you schedule an abortion for Saturday? I'll go with you and then stay with you Saturday night to make sure you're okay."

"I don't know, Ron," she cried. "I need some time to think. What about adoption?"

"Not a good idea, Jen. If the kid comes out less than perfect, you're back to square one and stuck with it. We can't talk about this on the phone. I'll come right from the airport to your place Friday night. In fact, schedule the abortion and I'll stay with you both Friday and Saturday—and Sunday, if you need me to."

"I. . .can't see you Friday, Ron." Jenna was feeling trapped. Trapped between a baby and an abortion and trapped between Ron and Brian.

"You tell me you're pregnant and then say you can't see me? Come on, Jenna!"

"You don't know what this is like for me, Ron. My whole life has been turned upside down in less than a day!" she protested. Another pause.

"I'm sorry, babe," he said so gently that Jenna's tears came harder. "I'm sorry for yelling. This just wasn't what I expected, you know?" She heard him exhale slowly. "Make the appointment for Saturday and don't worry about the cost. Throw away all that junk you got at that place. It'll only make this all the harder. I'll be there Friday, okay?"

Jenna stared at the blank screen of her television after they hung up. What was she going to do? She hadn't had a blood test yet, but she knew she was pregnant. She knew it. She also knew Ron would support her as long as she got an abortion. If she didn't, well, that would probably be another story. And now that Brian was back, she wasn't so sure Ron was whom she wanted. She knew Brian was—except that Brian was leaving the wife and kids he had already. If she had a child, would he leave her again?

"Please, God," she said, "If You take care of this, I promise I'll. . ."

Promise what? she thought. She turned on the television. This prayer stuff wasn't for her. She'd been solving her own problems her entire life. She could hardly go running to God when things got tough. She watched the program with blank eyes and couldn't recall later what she had even seen.

By Friday things had gone from bad to worse. Jenna was still sick every morning. She had been unable to make contact with Brian and she was fearful she would have both Brian and Ron at her door simultaneously. By the time her doorbell rang at seven-thirty, her anxiety had her stomach in knots.

Brian breezed in, pulling her quickly to him. Her lackluster response left him piqued. He held her at arm's length, his hand caressing her face. "That's not the greeting I expected, Jay."

"I haven't been feeling well," she said, her nerves frayed, her thoughts a jumble. "I tried to reach you to cancel tonight, but I couldn't."

"Remember what we used to do when either of us had had a bad day or long week at work?" he asked, not giving her time to respond. "Come on, let's take a slow walk and we'll come back and the world-famous massage therapist will work all that tension out of you."

Jenna started to protest, but Brian turned down the lights, turned the stereo on low, and helped her on with her coat.

"It will be a short walk."

"Brian, I can't. . ."

He shushed her with a kiss. "No argument. I'll give you the world's best massage and tuck you in as snug as a baby. No demands, no pressure, no interruptions."

Jenna did experience some relief as Brian held her close and walked with her around her neighborhood. His tales of the week lightened her anxiety somewhat, if only because of the distraction. He surprised her with a diamond necklace and talked about their future together.

True to his word, after their hand-in-hand walk, Brian began massaging Jenna's shoulders and back. He didn't speak; he didn't try to entice her into making love. Jenna felt the tension releasing its grip on her. When the telephone rang, Brian shushed her, shook his head, unplugged the phone, and kept rubbing her back. The soft music, warmth of the room, and Brian's gentle massage did what Brian said it would do and gave Jenna what she needed: sleep. She drifted into an exhausted, oblivious, dreamless sleep. She woke once during the night, but Brian was gone and the condo silent. She rolled over and fell back asleep immediately.

A demanding banging on her door shocked Jenna awake the next morning. For several seconds she couldn't get oriented. She reached for her robe and went to the door, hoping she wouldn't get sick before she had time to answer it. She yanked open the door to stop the incessant pounding, which was beginning to resonate in her head.

Ron almost knocked her down as he stomped into the room, his face a tight, angry mask. He looked like he hadn't slept. His shirt was disheveled, his hair unkempt, and his glasses in place instead of his contact lenses. Jenna was feeling angry herself for having her blissful sleep disrupted by Ron's early, unannounced visit.

"There's nothing the matter with the doorbell, you know," she said coldly.

"Is that so?" he retorted. "It didn't seem to be working last night—or did you just choose not to answer it?"

Jenna shut the door and faced him, all the pieces of the evening before coming back to her. "I went to take a walk," she said, her defenses rising.

"A *walk?* Be real, Jen. You don't even walk a half-block to the carryout!" He paced the living room like a caged animal. Jenna had never seen Ron so angry. "Your phone didn't seem to be in working order last night either—or did you choose not to answer it?"

Jenna sat down on the sofa, afraid that nausea was going to overcome her any second. "Maybe it's not working," she offered, somewhat mollified.

"And maybe Death Valley will freeze over in the next ten minutes," he countered.

An equally biting response came to Jenna's mind, but suddenly Ron seemed to wilt. His shoulders drooped, he removed his glasses to rub his eyes, and he dropped into the chair. He looked at Jenna intently, his scrutiny silencing her angry retort. He gestured to the roses that looked as limp as he now did.

"Those flowers weren't from your dad, were they, Jen?" he asked quietly.

"Yes, they—"

"Don't lie to me, Jen!" His brief crescendo ended abruptly. "I don't like being lied to," he said in a more controlled voice. He looked down at his hands and put his glasses back on. "I called Garth last night," he said.

Garth? What has Garth got to do with anything? she wondered.

"I asked him," Ron continued, "if a sports car with a license plate reading FLYBOY meant anything to him."

Jenna felt like she had been slapped. Garth had told Ron about Brian. She couldn't think of a response. Ron walked to the piano and ran his fingers skillfully up the keyboard.

"So whose baby is it really, Jenna?" he asked quietly. "Or don't you even know?"

"I. . .I'm telling you the truth, Ron. This is your. . .our baby," she corrected herself. "Brian just came here last week for the first time in two years. I hadn't seen him until last Saturday."

Ron's look was a mix of disdain and skepticism. "So you haven't been sleeping with him too?" he asked. Jenna hesitated; she couldn't think fast enough. Her lack of a ready response gave Ron the answer he suspected. "So I figured," he said with a mirthless laugh. An oppressive silence filled the next few seconds. Jenna didn't know what to say.

"Why come to me with stories that this is my kid, Jen? Your 'Flyboy' has considerably more money than I do at this point. Why not hit him up with the bill? Afraid of scaring him off?"

"It's not like you think, Ron," she said, fighting back tears and her queasy stomach. She was afraid any explanation she attempted would only make things worse. Ron turned away from her to look out the window. His voice was low and pain-filled.

"I've loved you, Jenna. Before you I never. . .well, I've never slept with another woman. I thought maybe we could move in together—I was willing to make that commitment." He turned to face her and the tears in his eyes brought the same to Jenna's. "But this guy has some hold on you, Jen. Garth told me how it was with you when you first met this guy. I got over knowing you used to be involved with Garth, but. . ." He stopped and took a breath. "But I don't know how to compete with this guy, Jen. I've never told you this, but I've heard you speak his name in your sleep. When Garth told me his name last night, I put it all together. I don't want this baby, Jenna, or any other baby. Like I said, it's not in my game plan. And I could never be sure if it was even mine, no matter what you told me. I'm not paying for the abortion, Jenna. I'm not paying for anything. If you want to keep this baby, that's your business. But don't be calling me for blood testing or with a paternity suit or any of that. Don't humiliate me and don't degrade yourself any more than you already have." There was still a hint of tears in Ron's eyes, but his chin was set and his look chilling. "How could you do this, Jenna? How could you?"

Jenna wanted to say something, anything. But no words would come. She wanted to tell him she was sorry, that this really was his baby. But she couldn't speak. He shook his head and walked to the door, turning to face her once more before leaving.

"Good-bye, Jenna. Don't call me when you and the Flyboy crash-land."

He finalized his last, bitter remark with a slamming of the door behind him.

Jenna's tears became anguished sobs. How had she gotten herself into this mess? How could she get out of it? She had started to love Ron—and she hadn't *asked* for Brian to come back into her life! She looked at the telephone. She had to talk to Brian. Jenna almost lost her resolve when a woman answered Brian's home number.

"Is Brian there, please?" she asked. The reply was terse.

"He doesn't live here anymore."

Jenna put the receiver down. So Brian was telling the truth. He had left Caroline. But that did little to lighten her aching heart or quell her stomach. She wasn't sure of anything anymore: her feelings about Ron or Brian or the pregnancy. She just wanted out of the whole mess.

Ten miserable days later, Jenna's "whole mess" had been resolved. The pregnancy was what her doctor called a tubal ectopic: Surgery was necessary and the end result was that she was no longer pregnant. Jenna was almost ecstatic, in spite of the nurse's warning that there might be some emotional backlash from her loss, as she called it. *Loss?* Jenna thought. *I'm free! No abortion! No baby!* She could pick up where she left off two years ago—no, it was better than that. Not only did she no longer have to consider Ron; there was no Caroline either! It could just be her and Brian. They could start fresh.

Brian called her to tell her he would be out of town another week, but he was looking forward to their time together. Jenna was thinking of having a candlelight dinner together, or going to the theater, or spending time making plans for their new future together. After a few minutes on the telephone with Brian, however, it was clear he only had one thing on his mind and it had nothing to do with dinner or the theater.

"Is that all you can think of, Brian?" Jenna asked, trying to remember if her doctor had said anything about that after her surgery.

"When it comes to you, Jay," he answered, "yes!" He obviously found his comment amusing, because he had laughed. Jenna neither laughed nor smiled. The conversation left her unsettled and wondering about Brian's true feelings for her. What was the matter with her? Brian was just being Brian. That had always been an integral part of their relationship. Why was she having doubts now when she was free of Ron and pregnancy? The harsh ring of her telephone startled her.

"Jenna? This is Barb from the Crisis Pregnancy Center. I was calling to see how you're doing."

"Oh, hi. Fine, thanks," she answered.

"Have you seen a doctor yet?"

"Uh, yes. I had an ectopic pregnancy and had to have surgery, so I'm not pregnant anymore."

"I'm sorry. How are you feeling?"

"Very glad not to be pregnant! I'm glad I didn't have to make a big decision, if you know what I mean. My. . .uh. . .boyfriend really didn't want a baby."

"So your life is all back together now? Everything's all right?"

"Well," Jenna's throat constricted and a fresh round of tears began. "Well, I. . .uh. . .things are better, of course, now that there's no baby." She looked down at her abdomen and ran her hand gently across it.

There was no baby.

"Listen, I've got to go. Thanks for calling." Jenna didn't listen for a good-bye and hung up. She was going to have a major pity party if she didn't get out of her apartment and do something! She would give her twin sister the surprise of her life and drop in unannounced. Maybe the thirty-mile drive would help her get her head together.

So that was how Jenna ended up at her sister's. It didn't take Janet long to see something was troubling her twin. She had lost weight and the dark circles under her eyes were from more than her smeared mascara. Although their relationship had been somewhat strained over the past several years, it wasn't long before Jenna, in bits and pieces, had told Janet most of what had happened in the last few weeks.

Janet had to restrain herself when Jenna told her she had started "seeing Brian again." Janet well remembered Brian. His inflated ego was matched only by his hyperactive libido. The one time she had met him when he and Jenna were having their affair, she knew Brian was nothing but a flirt. His condescending air and lecherous scrutiny of every woman that walked by him told Janet two things: One, Brian was nothing more than a womanizer, and two, he liked women at least half his age. She personally couldn't tolerate the man. What in the world Jenna saw in him was beyond her.

It was obvious now, however, that Jenna's lifelong party had come to an end. Although she still seemed oblivious to the real Brian, the reckless abandon with which Jenna had always breezed through her life was gone. Between Brian's ill-timed arrival back into Jenna's life, Ron's abrupt departure from it, and the pregnancy and surgery, it was clear her sister was emotionally spent. Janet hurt for her, but hoped that now Jenna was ready to learn about a better way to live—a real way, a fulfilling way.

"I don't understand it, Janny. I'm no longer pregnant, Ron is gone, and Brian is free and back," Jenna mused aloud. "Everything should be fine now, but nothing is. And where God fits in to all of it, I have no clue." She sighed and gazed out the window.

"Jenny," Jan continued, using her childhood name for her twin, "Jesus came to earth to show us how to please God. He died on the cross so we would have the power to do that. In living for God, we find answers for our lives in relationship to others as well as Him. You tell me you've done nothing to please God. Have you done anything that even pleases you?"

After a few moments Jenna shook her head in resignation.

"Perhaps, Jen, you're beginning to see your need for Jesus Christ," Janet said quietly.

"So we are back to where we started," Jenna said, almost inaudibly.

"Yes, but you can start again, Jenny. The Bible tells us that

Jesus came into the world to save sinners—and that we are all sinners."

Jenna shook her head again. "Not you, Jan. You wouldn't know a sin if it bit you. You were the perfect pastor's wife before you were even married."

"That's not true, Jenny, and you know it. I've had my sins and you've had yours. The point is that we both need God's forgiveness, and the beauty of it is that He offers us just that through Jesus Christ. But we can't make excuses. We must repent of our sin, ask the Lord's forgiveness, and then seek to live a life that pleases Him. Not out of a sense of earning His goodwill, but out of gratitude for giving us a life that Jesus calls 'abundant' and 'true.' "

"I want that, Jan. I want what you and Matt have, but I don't even go to church!"

"It's not about going to church; it's about praying. Praying and asking God to forgive you and believing that He will. You have only to ask, Jen. Jesus said all who seek Him will find Him when they seek with all their heart. Let me pray with you, Jenna. It's time you gave your life back to the One who gives you life."

This time Jenna did not watch the person who prayed for her, but prayed herself, following her sister's lead. Janet had taken both Jenna's hands in hers; Jenna didn't know if it were her tears or her sister's that fell on her fingers—or the tears of both of them.

"Dear Lord," Janet began, "You know Jenna and have loved her since before she was born. You know the life she has lived and the person she has been, but still You have loved her. You want her to surrender her life to You and we know You make no other demands other than that she humbly repent and receive your gift of life—your gift of eternal life." Janet hesitated and then said, "Pray after me, Jenna."

Jenna held her hands tighter.

"Dear Lord, I know that I'm a sinner."

" 'Dear Lord, I know that I'm a sinner,' " Jenna repeated.

"Forgive me for all my sin."

" 'Forgive me for all my sin, please,' " Jenna prayed earnestly.

"I receive you now as my Savior and Lord." Jenna repeated the words. "And thank You for saving me from my sins."

" 'And thank You for saving me from my sins.' "

"Help me to live the rest of my life for You."

Jenna again repeated the words and then listened as her sister prayed once more.

"Lord God, how I have prayed for this moment! Thank You! Thank You!" she whispered. "Would you like to say anything else, Jenny?" she asked. Jenna didn't answer, but continued to pray.

"Thank You, Lord, too. I don't know what all this means yet, but thank You. And help me with Brian. Help me to know what to do. Amen."

"Amen," Janet repeated. She looked at her sister through joyful tears and hugged her tightly. "My dear, dear sister in every sense of the word," she said.

Jenna saw no bright lights, no visions. But the calm peace that pushed out the heartache and disquietude was so powerful that it defied description. She felt free somehow—and clean—and whole. But the peace and the humility were sensations so new to her as to be almost overwhelming.

"I can't tell you all I'm feeling right now, Janny," she said. "It's like I've come out from under a weight that I didn't even know was there until it was gone!" She felt almost giddy with the reality of it. "Will I always feel like this?" she asked.

"I'm afraid not," Janet said, wiping her red eyes and hugging her sister again. "Sometimes you'll wonder if you just imagined this moment. Life still deals some hard blows and there will be times when you think the Lord is nowhere to be found. But He tells us in the Bible He will never leave us or forsake us. And that's what you stake your faith on—not on whatever you are or aren't feeling at the moment." She pulled her sister to her feet. "Come on. Let's get you into your first Bible study."

"Over hot fudge sundaes and coffee?" Jenna asked, suddenly hungry.

"I can't think of a better combination!" Janet laughed and they walked to her kitchen arm in arm, just as they had so often as little girls.

The initial days of Jenna's new life were marked by some radical changes. Some things, it seemed, she knew instinctively: clothes that weren't proper attire or novels she had and promptly threw away. She began examining things she had never thought twice about before: television programs or attitudes purported in some women's magazines she had followed unquestioningly for years. Business practices at work. It was like she was seeing life through Another's eyes. It was all new for Jenna, refreshing, but disconcerting. But the new peace she awoke with day after day overshadowed it all.

In spite of the long drive, she began attending a ladies' Bible study with Janet. She started going to a church near her home that her brother-in-law had recommended. She no longer wondered about the kind of person she was; she knew what kind of person she had been. And she was determined, with the Lord's help, to be different. She wanted to be different. She had read in the Gospel of John that Jesus said "You must be born again." What a perfect expression! That was just how she felt! She used to poke fun at her sister and Matt as "born-againers." She wasn't making fun at their expense anymore; she was reveling in the fact of new spiritual birth herself.

Then the package came from Brian.

She was afraid to open it. Earlier that week he had sent her a gift, and it had made her blush even though she was home alone. She would not have blushed a year ago. But a lot had happened since she last saw Brian just a few short weeks ago. She had thrown the indecent gift into the trash and prayed for an hour afterwards. Now she sat on her sofa again, another gift from Brian on her lap. This one at least had a card; the last had not.

"Jay," it read, "Can't wait to see you. I love and miss you. Brian." She couldn't stop the sudden beating of her heart and slowly opened the box. A small, exquisite bottle of perfume she hadn't worn in years (only because she couldn't afford it) was his gift. It was so thoughtful! He had remembered after all this time! For the first time in weeks, she longed for Brian, for his arms around her and the gentle possessiveness of his eyes on her. She didn't know if she should want or miss Brian, but suddenly she did. Her dreams of him that night were tender, sweet, and pleasant. She decided it was the fragrance of the perfume that triggered them.

The telephone, her ever-dependable wake-up call, rang early the next morning.

"Hello?" she said, her voice groggy with sleep.

"Jay, sweetheart. Sorry to call so early. Your answering machine hasn't been working and I haven't been able to get ahold of you." Jenna was immediately awake.

"I've been spending some time with my sister and. . .some other friends," she finished lamely.

"I just called to say I miss you, Jay. I should be home in a day or so. Did you get the gifts I sent?"

She swallowed. What would he do or say when he found out she'd thrown out the first one?

"Yes. Thank you especially for the perfume. You really shouldn't have, Brian."

"Hey! Nothing's too good for my favorite girl," he said. She expected the usual innuendo, especially when she said nothing about the first gift he had sent, but it didn't come.

"What do you say we do it up big when I come back? Go to a new restaurant, take in a play—what do you say?"

"That sounds wonderful, Brian," she said.

"You're wonderful, Jay," he said, as lovingly as anything he'd ever said to her. "I'll see you Friday, baby doll."

Jenna stretched out on her bed, wide awake and smiling. No innuendo! No teasing, suggestive laughter! He did love and miss her for herself! And he wasn't married to Caroline anymore—not really, anyway. She would tell Brian about becoming a Christian—and maybe he would pray with her just like she had prayed with Janet! Perhaps, she thought, his divorce from Caroline was God's will, a phrase that she often heard now in her new, growing circle of Christian friends. That way Brian could be saved like she was and they could be married! She would be a good stepmother to his children. Before she got ready for work, she prayed.

"Thank You, Lord," she said happily. But she remembered the trashed gift and her past with Brian and finished more somberly. "But help me do the right thing."

As Jenna waited for Brian's arrival Friday, Janet called her.

"Hi! What are you up to tonight?" she asked.

"Brian is coming home today," Jenna replied, but then

continued quickly. "He said something about taking in a play tonight." There was silence on the other end of the line. Jenna feared what her sister might say—that a rebuke was coming. "You think it's okay if I see him, don't you?" she asked. "I mean," she hurried on to say, "he is separated from Caroline now."

"Jen. . ." Janet hesitated a moment more. "I don't know if you're ready to face him yet, Jenna. You know how persuasive Brian can be."

"But we really do love each other, Jan. I think he'll respect my feelings now about. . .well, you know. . ." Jenna felt embarrassed talking to her sister about Brian, and wasn't sure why she was.

"About chastity?" Janet finished for her. She didn't wait for a response. "Don't count on it, Jenna. Listen, the Spirit of God lives in you now. You don't have to ask me about issues like this. Seek the Lord and ask Him what you should do. But I will say this, and I say it lovingly and carefully. . ." She paused again. "Brian is still a married man. Your love for him or his for you does not change that fact. But even if he were not still married, you still have an obligation to moral purity because God calls us to it. I. . .really don't think you should see him yet," she said.

Jenna immediately felt defensive, but what was there to defend? Her sister was right, but she didn't know Brian like she did. She had never seen Brian's tender side—the part of him that was searching for more, just as she had been. She was just about to say all this when the doorbell rang.

"I've got to go, Jan. I'll think about what you said."

"Matt and I will be praying for you, Jenny. I know this is going to be hard for you. But pray—and be ready to obey the Lord."

Jenna nervously, excitedly, prayerfully went to the door. She glanced in her mirror for a last-minute check and opened the door. Brian, handsome, smiling, his tie loosened and a large gift box of more roses under his arm, strolled into the room. He wasted no time pulling Jenna against him for a lingering kiss. Jenna's pulse raced and she eagerly returned his kiss.

"Hello, Jay. You look good enough to eat! Brought you something. . ." He held the satiny box out to her. The array of roses was beautiful; their fragrance was intoxicating.

"They're beautiful, Brian. Thank you." She took them to the kitchen while Brian removed his tie and coat. As Jenna placed each rose into a vase, she had a sickening premonition of history repeating itself. This was just how it all started with Brian last month.

"I need a shower, Jay," he announced. "Give me a few minutes to clean up." He grabbed a towel and washcloth from her linen closet. "Would you mind grabbing my suitcase out of my car? Just set it inside the bathroom door."

He shut the door behind him and Jenna sank to the chair in prayer. She was shaking. "Help me, Lord," was all she could pray. She retrieved his suitcase and did as he had asked. She tried to busy herself while Brian showered, but she began to have a sinking feeling about the evening ahead. Where was the peace she had been enjoying for the last few weeks? Did it go out the door when Brian came in? Maybe it had just been the result of her surgery and the stress of the last. . .

No. The peace is real and genuine, she reminded herself. Her new faith was real and the Lord was with her—she had read that for herself. She relaxed somewhat more when Brian emerged from the bathroom fully dressed. He sat down on the sofa across from her.

"Ahhh," he said, "I feel like a new man." Jenna regarded him with mingled attraction and dread. Brian returned her look with bold scrutiny. She felt ill at ease and almost frightened.

This can't be happening again, she thought.

"Were you able to get some theater tickets?" she asked.

"No, sorry, I forgot. How about a movie?"

"Maybe we should talk," she ventured.

"Talk?" he snorted. "What is it with all this 'talk' stuff lately? Come over here and sit beside me." He patted the sofa next to him. Jenna walked over timidly. He pulled her to him for a kiss, but this time Jenna did not return his passion. He sensed it immediately. He released her and leaned back again. "So what's the problem? Seeing your other boyfriend again?"

"There's no 'other boyfriend,' Brian." She paused. "Something happened to me while you were gone."

"Oh?" He barely covered a yawn and began rubbing the back of her neck. "What's that?" he asked with little interest.

Jenna got up to get away from his touch. He let his hand hit his leg with a slap. "Well, what is it you want to talk about, Jay? I've had a long day in the sky."

"I. . .I've been saved. I'm a born-again Christian now." There. She had said it. Brian got up, grabbed a can of diet pop from her refrigerator, and opened the can. He smiled patronizingly at her and took a drink of his soda.

"So you're a Holy Roller now? A Bible-toting moralizer out to save the world?" He took another drink and plopped back down on the sofa. "Come on, Jay. This is the real world."

"This is real too, Brian. It's almost like something I can't describe," she said, feeling frustrated by her ineptness.

He shrugged. "Fine. So what? You go to church on Sunday now. I'll be working or sleeping in. What's that got to do with us?"

"Well, it has. . .everything to do with us," she said weakly. She wanted him to understand so badly, but she didn't know how to make him understand. "I. . .we. . ." she was stammering and she knew it. He came to her and wrapped his arms around her.

"Hey! I think I like this 'new Jay' now," he said teasingly. "Soft-spoken, docile, compliant. . ." She pulled out of his embrace. "Well, maybe not compliant," he chuckled. He saw her look and changed tactics.

"Okay, okay. What is it? Caroline? That's over, Jay! It's just you and me now!"

"It's not just Caroline, Brian. You. . .you're not a Christian like I am now."

"Yes, I am!" he said with a chuckle. "I've been a Christian all my life! I believe in God and all that stuff! Doesn't the Bible say God is love?" He reached for his can of soda and gestured with it in hand. "Well, I love you and you love me and God loves us and that's all there is to it, right?"

Jenna raised her hand to rub her forehead. Brian was talking in circles and she was afraid she wasn't making any sense either. Brian took another step towards her, but she backed away. She needed time—and space—to think.

"We can talk about this later, Jay," he said in a conciliatory tone. He kept coming to her, but she backed away again.

"It's not going to be like this anymore, Brian," she said.

He mumbled an obscenity and returned to the chair. "Listen, Jenna," he said. Jenna never remembered him calling her by her given name. "I didn't fly back across the country today to indulge you in some 'let's play hard to get' game."

"It's not a game, Brian. It never was."

For the first time since she had known him, Jenna saw Brian as her sister saw him. She didn't know where the next question she threw at him came from.

"What's her name, Brian? The other woman you've been sleeping with."

Brian looked at Jenna with guarded uncertainty. "How do you know about her?" he asked. No denial—no "What woman?"

He didn't even appear offended by her question. He shrugged his shoulders and drank the last of his beverage.

"She's nothing to me, Jay. It was just one of those things."

Is that all I've ever been? "Just one of those things"? she wondered.

"And the others?" she asked, pushing her sudden advantage.

"Warm bodies for cold nights," he grumbled. "Hey! What is this? The third degree? You sound like Caroline, for Pete's sake." He threw the can in the garbage.

Jenna couldn't believe what she had just heard. She had always thought she had been the "other woman." The sudden realization that she was just one of. . .who knew how many "other" women made her reach for the chair and sit down. She had never meant anything more—or less—to Brian than Caroline, or any other woman! He returned her disbelieving stare with a roll of his eyes.

"So what's the problem? I'm here with you now and it will be you and me from here on in. You know what it's like sometimes, Jay. That was your boyfriend who stopped by and then called the last time I was here, wasn't it?"

She didn't know how he knew about Ron, but it didn't matter now. "That was different," she said with some shame.

Brian's laugh was derisive. "Yeah, right. Enough of this *talk*. Let's go get supper."

Jenna's heart ached. This is how it was with Brian. How it would always be with Brian. He would never be any more faithful to her than he had been to Caroline. He was no more a Christian than she had been. She was not special to him. She had wasted years of her life on a man who cared no more for her than for. . .any other "warm body on a cold night."

Brian sensed the change in Jenna and came to stand before her. "I'm sorry, Jay. There won't be any other women anymore. You know I love only you," he said gently.

"No, Brian, I don't know that."

"Is it this religion thing? If you want, I'll go to church with you every Sunday. I promise you there won't be any others, Jay."

"Your promise isn't enough, Brian."

He thought a moment and matched Jenna's intense gaze. His next words were not spoken harshly or angrily, but evenly and deliberately.

"If I walk out that door now, Jay, I'll never walk back through it again."

Tears came to Jenna's eyes, but her voice was resolute. "Goodbye, Brian," was all she said.

Brian gathered his suitcase and keys. He walked out the door quietly without a backward glance. Jenna sat alone in the darkening room and stared at the fresh roses on the piano. The realization of what had just transpired stole over her. For the first time, she had not given in to Brian! She knew that, strange as it was, for some reason she still loved him. But she knew she was free of him too. And the freedom *from* him was better than the love she had had with him.

"Thank You, Lord," she whispered into the darkness.

Jenna called her twin sister before eight o'clock the next morning.

"Hi, Jan," was all she got out before Janet cut her off.

"How did it go?" Jan asked without preamble.

"You were praying for me, weren't you?" Jenna asked in return, a new confidence in her voice.

"Like my life depended on it!" Jan exclaimed.

"Well, it's over. Really over for good."

"Praise God," Jan said quietly. "Want to talk about it?"

"I think I do. Can you come by tomorrow?"

"Tomorrow nothing! I'm leaving now! Put on the coffee!"

Jenna hung up the telephone and went to make some

coffee. She looked outside. The newborn day hinted of good days to come. She was newly born too. It was an exhilarating beginning!

CHAPTER 8

Stepping Back

Man looks at the outward appearance,
but the LORD looks at the heart.
—1 Samuel 16:7 NIV

Maggie Jensen dropped the simple, fitted black dress down over her slight frame and slipped her feet into her black heels. Before putting on the last of her makeup and her jewelry, she sat on the corner of the bed that had been hers during her growing-up years. She picked up the invitation on the bedspread beside her. Her fifteenth high school class reunion! She couldn't believe it. She hadn't made the fifth; she was in a friend's wedding in another state. For the ten-year reunion she had a new job and couldn't get the time off to come. But for number fifteen, she had made it!

She had left the sultry heat of Dallas that morning, promising herself she would not check her voice mail until Tuesday at the earliest. She was going to be seventeen again this weekend! She was going to wallow in memories, catch up with old friends, and find out what happened to her last high school heartthrob.

Dale Marciniak was his name. She had lost track of him and countless others. The one friend from high school she had maintained ties with, Cheryl, had been corresponding via E-mail with Maggie for years. But aside from Cheryl, Maggie had no idea what had become of most of her former classmates.

"Maybe I'll find out tonight!" Maggie said aloud. She had lived in three different states since graduating from college, none of them her home state of Michigan. It felt good to be home again, especially at some time other than Christmas. She had enjoyed the last two days with her family, but now it was time to get reacquainted with old friends. She reached for her hairbrush in anticipation of the evening ahead.

That evening Maggie got out of her rental car and paused to look at the banquet hall she would be entering. Her senior prom had been held here. It had been her last date with Dale. That memory was not a happy one. . . .

"Why don't we leave now, Maggie? Jeff's folks are gone and a bunch of us are going over to his house to do some serious partying, if you catch my drift." Dale looked at her from across the table. They had only been at the prom for an hour or so.

"Leave now? No way! I've looked forward to this prom all year and I'm going to be the last one to leave!" Maggie protested. She was mad at Dale. He smelled like cigarettes; she suspected he had gone outside not because he "forgot something," but to have a smoke. She hated the smell of cigarettes. She thought she detected alcohol on his breath too when they were dancing. That scared her. She had never drunk alcohol and neither did her parents. Her dad, a police officer, was always ranting and raving about drunk drivers and brawls at bars. He threatened to ground Maggie for life if he ever caught her drinking. She took his threat seriously. Dale's look and angry response cut short young Maggie's thoughts.

"You're being a drag, Mags," he said, perturbed.

"Forget it, Dale! This is our senior prom! I plan to stay for the entire evening." Maggie picked up her sequined purse. "I'm going to freshen up my makeup. I'll be right back," she told him. She didn't want him or anyone else to see she was close to tears. He was going to spoil everything if he kept insisting they leave the prom early! And it would only get her in trouble with her folks if they did!

Maggie came out of her brief reminiscing. She had stayed the entire evening. Alone. Dale left while she had gone to freshen up. She had spent the remainder of the prom with her dateless girlfriends and not with her date. She and Dale had never spoken to each other the rest of the school year. He found a new girlfriend. Maggie simply endured the rest of the year, hurt and angry that he had ruined her long-anticipated senior prom and had humiliated her all in one evening. She smiled now. She had survived the heartbreak and the humiliation, in spite of her conviction back then that she would do neither. She pulled her coat more tightly around herself and walked to the entrance. She hoped this trip to Jacobsen's Banquet Hall would prove an improvement over that last time here! Once inside the building, she hung up her coat and looked inquisitively around the room for Cheryl.

"Mags! You made it! When I didn't hear from you today, I was afraid you didn't come after all." Maggie hadn't seen Cheryl in two years, but she looked as attractive as ever. She returned her friend's enthusiastic hug.

"Motherhood agrees with you, Cheryl. You look great. You brought pictures of the kids, I hope."

"Of course! I hope you can come over and see them in person while you're home. You look sensational, Maggie. That dress is perfect on you! Our table is full now that you're here. Wait until you see everyone!"

The next hour was a whirl of excited greetings and catching up. Maggie couldn't get over how some of her former classmates had changed so much, and how others had changed so little. Most of her friends were married now, a couple were divorced and remarried, and a few were single like her. She enjoyed looking at pictures of children and hearing about the high points of her old friends' lives. She and her friend, Marcia, were just remembering the "sleepover to end all sleepovers" when she felt a tap on her shoulder.

"Hello, Maggie."

"Dale?" She stood to receive and return a friendly hug from the handsome man before her. Dale was taller than she remembered him. His air and appearance emanated confidence, wealth, and control. He looked like a walking advertisement for the *Man of Today* magazine. Dale could possibly be the most attractive man Maggie had ever seen. "It took me a split second to recognize you," she said, hoping she wasn't blushing like a schoolgirl.

Dale stood at the table for a few minutes greeting everyone and getting into a brief discussion with two men on the latest bull stock market. Maggie and Marcia had taken up their topic of their last high school sleepover again, but Dale touched Maggie's arm.

"Join me at my table for a few minutes?" he asked, but he had already started to direct her to another table. She asked Marcia to keep an eye on her purse and allowed Dale to lead her across the room. He indicated a chair for her to sit down and sat across from her, his back to the dance floor. He seemed to want to talk to her alone. Maggie was flattered, but she also felt a little shy. And she never felt shy!

"Well," he said, setting down his beverage.

"Well yourself," she said, working to appear relaxed. "I

haven't seen you since. . ."

"Graduation," he finished for her. "And we haven't talked since I left you at our homecoming dance or the senior prom or something." His smile was teasing and not at all apologetic.

"It was the senior prom," she answered. "In fact, it was here."

She couldn't read his smile; it seemed remote somehow. "Do you always remember things in such detail?" he asked.

"Yes. At least, some things." She met his penetrating gaze and saw the smile make its way to his eyes.

"I'm sorry about that, Maggie. It was rude of me. I was young and somewhat stupid then." He slowly turned his glass around on the table. He didn't seem to be struggling for words at all, just taking his time as he quietly assessed her. *He's a man used to being in charge,* she thought. She was sure he was never "rude" or "stupid" now. She suspected all his words and moves were carefully measured. Like a seasoned politician, or a calculating business magnate. She wondered if he could read her mind. He leaned back, assuming a more relaxed position. His penetrating, dark eyes never left her face.

"Fifteen years is a long time to wait for an apology, however," he conceded, now looking more contrite. "You're a beautiful woman now, Maggie. Too beautiful for 'Mags,' " he said. Maggie wasn't sure how to respond, so she lowered her eyes and took a drink of her beverage.

"So, catch me up on your life, Maggie," he said. "It looks like you're here alone. Are you married? Are you still living here in town? What's your line of work? Give me the last fifteen years in a nutshell."

"I live in Dallas—no, that's wrong," she corrected herself. "My apartment is in Dallas; I live out of my suitcase. I'm a clinical specialist for a large medical equipment company. I'm not married—"

"Divorced?" he interrupted, still turning his glass around on the table.

"Uh. . .no," she stumbled. "Just single." She took a breath and continued. "I attend a large church in Dallas where I've just starting going since I became a Christian. I enjoy aerobics and fencing—"

"Fencing!" He laughed, not in derision, but mirth. "How did you ever become interested in fencing?"

"I took it in college and enjoyed it so much that I stayed with it. That, the aerobics, and racquetball are my exercise outlets."

"I enjoy racquetball too."

"What is your line of work now?" she asked. "That's about all there is to tell about me. Your turn." She self-consciously smoothed back her russet hair.

"Promise you won't laugh," he said. His study of her made her acutely aware that she wouldn't laugh—even if he said he were a comedian by profession. "I always preface my response with the fact that my career has been very good for me financially and personally. I'm a professional model. Magazines, television commercials, that sort of thing."

"Really? What do you advertise?" No wonder he looked like he'd just stepped out of a gentleman's European style show or the *Man of Today* magazine! He probably had! Had she seen him in any magazine or television ads and not recognized him?

"Whatever they ask me to advertise, as long as the price is right," he said in response to her question. "Fragrances, clothing, sporting goods, you can just about name it and I've been the face and/or body to try and sell it."

"You know, now that you tell me this. . ." Maggie thought a minute. "Have you done ads for Highlander jeans?"

"As a matter of fact, I have," he answered.

"And were you in some TV commercial for business machines

or something recently?" He nodded his head affirmatively. "You know, I thought you looked familiar! But I just blew it off! This is amazing!"

"As I recall, for the one they put a black wig on me and for the other I had to grow a beard and wear glasses instead of my contact lenses."

"Maybe I should be asking for your autograph!" No wonder Dale looked like a movie star; he almost was one! "It must be an exciting career," she said, fascinated.

"Not really. Early morning hours, long, boring stretches between shots, jet lag that dogs my steps for days at a time," he confessed. "And not much time to build lasting relationships," he said more quietly.

"I can appreciate some of those things," Maggie concurred, choosing to avoid his last statement and penetrating look. "I can't tell you how many times my luggage has been lost or I've been stuck in airports." She took another drink of her beverage; her throat felt dry.

"No kids?" he asked, forcing the conversation back to a more personal note.

There was a time, she thought, *when my answer to his questions about my marital status would have been the obvious answer to this question. Not anymore, I guess.* "No. You?" she asked.

"I have a son by a previous marriage and a daughter by my second marriage. My second divorce was final some months ago."

"I'm sorry," she offered.

"Don't be. I'm not. I see Heather and Jeremy fairly regularly." He reached for his wallet. "Like to see pictures?"

"Of course." She looked at the two pictures while Dale continued talking.

"Jeremy is ten now and Heather is four. He lives in southern California with his mother and stepdad. Heather and her mother live in New Jersey."

"They're beautiful children, Dale. How you must miss them! How often do you get to see them?" she asked, handing the photographs back to him.

"Twice. . .three times a year," he said casually, replacing his wallet.

That's fairly regularly? she thought to herself. "How can you stand it?"

"That's just the way life is. I'm pretty busy with my work. Always have been. Ashley would tell you I don't see Heather any less than I did when we were married." Maggie's face must have shown her surprise at his casual tone, because he raised his hand in self-defense. "But Ashley tends to exaggerate big-time. All the time. Especially when it comes to me."

Maggie wasn't sure how to respond to all this. She wanted to change the subject, but felt compelled to pursue it at the same time. At least in regards to Dale himself.

"Are you happy, Dale?" she asked.

"Sometimes. Are you?" he countered.

"Yes, I am," she said truthfully. "But before I became a Christian, my answer would have been the same as yours."

"What do you mean by 'before I became a Christian'? You and your family went to church, didn't you? I never made that claim even as a kid; we didn't go to church." He continued to move his glass in a circle on the table.

"Yes, we did go to church. But I didn't have an intimate, genuine relationship with Jesus Christ. Church was just church. It wasn't going to a place to pray with other people or praise the Lord with other people. It was just something we did on most Sundays."

"Oh," he said with little enthusiasm. "Well, that's nice. Whatever works for you is the way to go, if you ask me. Whether you're one of the obnoxious 'religious right,' or a New Ager, or an agnostic—whatever works for the given individual is his or her course to chart."

"But what about truth?" Maggie asked. "Is pragmatism or feeling good the measure of a belief system's authenticity?"

"Hey! You're getting way out of my league, Magnolia Blossom!" he laughed. "Come back to earth!"

Magnolia Blossom. No one had ever called her that but Dale. She hated it fifteen years ago; now she found it almost laughable. She had forgotten that nickname he had given her. Before she could respond, a voice came over her shoulder.

"Hey! Dale! Ready to go?" A balding man Maggie didn't recognize came up to their table, interrupting their conversation. "What is this? A private party of some kind?" He looked at Maggie, sudden recognition dawning. "Maggie Jensen!" he exclaimed. "How are you?"

Maggie looked at his name tag and rose to shake his offered hand. "Harry! It's good to see you!"

"Whadaya think of our famous golden boy here, eh?" he asked, patting Dale's shoulder. He didn't wait for her response. "We need to get going, Dale. I'll bring the car around."

"I guess this is good-bye until our next reunion, Dale," she said, seeing that Dale had obviously made other plans for the evening. "It was nice talking with you again. I wish we had more time," Maggie said.

"Why don't you come with us?" he asked. "We were going to drive up to Windsor and hit the casino."

Maggie paused. She had never gambled in her life—not even a lottery ticket! Dale mistook her hesitation.

"I promise," he said smoothly, "I won't leave you there."

"The thought didn't even cross my mind, Dale." She smiled at him and Harry. "No thank you, but thanks for the invitation."

"Good seeing you, Maggie. I'll go get the car, Dale." Harry walked away from them.

"Where are you staying, Maggie? I'd like to call you before I fly out on Monday."

"At my parents' home. They're in the book."

"Sure you won't join us? It will be fun!"

"No, but thanks just the same." She turned to walk to her table, but Dale stepped up to her and touched his lips to her cheek.

"I'll call you," he whispered in her ear. Maggie felt a tingle that raced from her face to her feet. She hoped she wasn't flushed from his unexpected kiss when she sat down next to Marcia. She *felt* flushed.

"Is he a fox or what?" Marcia asked her so no one else could hear. "What did he say? You two looked pretty intent over there in the corner!"

"We didn't have much time to talk," Maggie said, somewhat evasively. "He said he'd call me tomorrow."

"Really?" Marcia asked. "This is sounding interesting! How could a guy who was just another jock in high school become a Greek god? He's better-looking than he was fifteen years ago, Maggie! And he's calling you? This is great!"

"I'm going to get another soft drink," Maggie said, standing again. She was embarrassed to be feeling so. . .starstruck. But her first attempt at sharing her new, personal relationship with Jesus Christ had certainly not gone very well. She raised her voice to take in the whole table. "Anyone else want something to drink?"

When everyone declined her offer, Maggie went to get her beverage. She was still trembling from her brief time with Dale. She had never had a model ask her for a date before! Well, he hadn't asked her for a date, but implied he would be calling her for just that. Her nervous excitement about going out with Dale, the "old boyfriend turned successful model," competed with her hesitancy about agreeing to see a man who had two failed marriages and was going out for an evening of gambling.

"Maggie?"

She turned to face a man with kind eyes who looked very uncomfortable just to have spoken her name. She looked at his name tag.

"Jim Gray?" She couldn't believe it was the same person! Jim Gray had sat next to her in her final history class. Jim had been a very overweight, painfully shy boy who was more at home under the hood of a car than he was with people. This man was not overweight; he was slender and not much taller than Maggie. She couldn't help but laugh.

"Is it really you, Jim? Or did you switch name tags with someone?"

He smiled the shy smile she well remembered. She had not seen it often on the face of the quiet, somber, essentially friendless teenager whom she had known years ago, but she recognized it.

"It is you! I wouldn't have known you in a hundred years!"

"I've managed to get out from under cars long enough to run off all those pounds that used to slow me down," he admitted. "It's easier to get under the cars this way too," he added, lowering his head briefly with a timid smile. "Do you have a few minutes to talk?" he asked.

"Sure, I'd love to. My table's pretty crowded—do you have room at yours?"

"Yes. It's over there near where you were sitting with Dale," he said, pointing.

"Let me grab my purse and I'll be right there," Maggie said. He nodded and turned to get a diet soda for himself.

Maggie excused herself from her friends once again.

"Cheryl, Marcia, I'm going to sit with Jim Gray for a few minutes, okay?"

"Jim who?" asked Cheryl, looking around to see who Maggie was talking about.

"You remember Jim Gray," she said, picking up her purse. "He used to work on cars all the time."

"Don't remember him," Cheryl replied with a shrug of her shoulders.

"Sure you do, Cheryl!" Marcia lowered her voice. "He was a great big gross guy with prescription ashtrays for glasses— you remember him! Is *he* going ask you out, too, Mags?"

Maggie didn't answer, but walked away with a tight smile. She remembered another time when she and Marcia had talked about Jim Gray. . .

"Could you go to the senior prom with me, Maggie?"

The heavy, perspiring boy before her shifted his weight self-consciously from foot to foot. His chin became two as he looked down to someplace between his beat-up tennis shoes. Others bustled by and around them on their way to their next classes.

"I'm sorry, Jim. I already have a date." That was a lie, but Maggie heard from more than one of her friends that Dale Marciniak was going to ask her to their prom. He had recently broken up with his steady girlfriend. "But thanks for asking," she ended, mentally congratulating herself for at least being gracious in her refusal. She dismissed the lying part as a half-truth. She didn't have a date yet, but she was sure she would have before the week was out. "Maybe some other time," she said, not really meaning it. Jim was nice and all, but she wasn't interested in dating him. Besides, what would her friends think?

"Oh. Okay," he mumbled, breaking into her thoughts. He

ambled away without looking back.

Marcia came up to Maggie. "What was that all about?" she asked, leading the way to their next class.

"Jim just asked me out," Maggie answered, again watching his slow, defeated retreat down the hallway. She felt kind of sorry for him. She knew it took a lot of courage for him to ask her out. He was afraid of his own shadow! And he was especially bashful around girls.

"That greasy slob?" Marcia cracked her gum. "Does he think you're major desperate for a date or something?" she asked, drawing her mouth up in disgust.

"Hey—he's a nice guy," Maggie said, rising to his defense. He had helped her more than once with geometry when they'd taken it together her sophomore year. And he had helped her in history class just last week after she'd been out sick for three days.

"Yeah. Right. A fat, greasy, gross 'nice guy.' Come on, we're going to be late for class." Marcia dragged Maggie down the hall at a slow run. Maggie looked back, but Jim was gone.

Maybe I will go out with him sometime! *Maggie thought.* If for no other reason than to spite Marcia and her sharp tongue!

That had been a long time ago. And Jim had never asked Maggie out again. Truth to be told, that was when she had eyes only for Dale, so it would have never happened anyway. Now Jim rose as she approached the table and pulled a chair out for her. She doubted he would have ever left her alone at the prom or anything else. He wasn't that kind of boy; she was sure he wasn't that kind of man either. She quickly greeted the other three people at the table, whom she barely remembered from high school. They talked briefly for a few minutes before Maggie was able to turn her complete attention back to Jim.

"So, tell me about yourself, Jim. Do you still live here in

town? Do you still work on cars or did you become a geometry teacher?" Maggie met his gaze with an encouraging smile. Jim dropped his eyes.

"Still live here. Still work on cars. I bought old man Fitch's place. Remember it?" he asked, looking up again.

"Of course! I can't remember how many times my friends and I would buy five bucks worth of gas—just enough to get us around in one evening!"

"A lot of kids did that. But you can't make much money selling five bucks worth of gas to kids on weekends. So the gas station is now an automotive repair shop. It keeps me busy. Most days I enjoy the work, although I usually put in a sixty-hour work week. How about you, Maggie?"

"I work out of Dallas for a medical equipment company. I've lived in Texas for the last six years," she replied.

"Do you like it?" he asked.

"Honestly?"

"Honestly."

"Not anymore. The traveling and company kudos were nice for a while, but I've grown weary of it. I like Dallas, but I miss southeast Michigan sometimes." She nibbled on some pretzels and her look was far away. "I might like Dallas better if I were able to spend more time there, but my traveling hasn't permitted it. Maybe it's time for a change."

"By coming back to where you started?" he prompted.

"Something like that," she smiled in reply. "Any outside interests? What do you really enjoy doing in your spare time?" she asked, her attention off herself and back on Jim.

"In the summer it's coaching little league baseball. In the fall and spring it's soccer. I also work with Triple J, a volunteer group of men from my church that take disadvantaged boys and mentor them. We get referrals from people and sometimes the court system. The boys are from broken homes, or are young guys who have had some early, minimal trouble with the law. We try to get them plugged into. . ." He stopped, apparently realizing he had said more words to Maggie in response to her simple question than he probably ever had! His smile was sheepish again and he finished quietly. "I really enjoy working with kids."

"That's quite obvious!" she said, encouraging him with a smile. She noticed his face had become animated and his speech less halting as he had warmed to the topic. "No children of your own?"

"No, not yet. I hope to have some someday."

He seemed not to know what to say next and sat with his eyes lowered. Maggie studied the angle of his jaw and the soft wave of his brown hair. He did not have Dale's polished, arresting appeal. But his unpretentious demeanor was charming. Perhaps because it was so rare in the few men she had dated in recent years. Someone waved at Maggie from another table and she returned the gesture. Jim saw it and immediately began apologizing.

"Am I keeping you from someone you want to talk to, Maggie? I don't mean to monopolize your evening."

"Not at all," she replied, determined to spend at least a few more minutes in the company of this man who had the direct opposite effect on her as Dale. She felt relaxed and at ease. Her pulse wasn't racing and she wasn't self-conscious to her toes. She felt like she had come home to an old friend. Maybe she had had enough of excitement from recent relationships that ended with her feeling like she had to take a backseat to someone's career, personal hang-ups, or fractured past relationships.

"Tell me more about your involvement at your church," she said.

"Well, in addition to the Triple J Ministry, I go overseas once or twice a year to help with construction projects that are part of my church denomination's missions ministry. I've helped build churches, dormitories, and outhouses." Maggie laughed and Jim smiled in mild embarrassment. "You wouldn't believe the alternative in some of those jungles!" His own laughter was more of a chuckle, but genuine. "I often work on the missionaries' cars, motor scooters, and motorcycles. I've worked on everything from brand-new luxury cars here in the USA to an old jalopy in Africa!"

"You and Dale Marciniak both have such fascinating careers!" she replied.

"My career isn't so fascinating, really, but these overseas trips are. It's not so much work for me as an opportunity to minister. I mean," he again seemed to realize he was talking a lot and spoke more haltingly. "That is. . .I feel like I can really make a difference for people in my own way. Like I feel with the Triple J."

"What does the 'J' stand for in that program?" Maggie asked.

"James, John, and Jesus. The man who started it got the idea from the close relationship between the two brothers—James and John—who were two of Jesus' closest friends and disciples. He applies it to us being like a big brother to some disadvantaged kid and building a close relationship with him and, hopefully, to point him to our great Elder Brother, Jesus Christ."

"That sounds neat. I became a Christian myself in just the last year. I went to a Christmas concert with a friend of mine at her church. At the end of the program the pastor talked about having a relationship with Jesus Christ. I had never heard anything quite like that before! I prayed later that night with my girlfriend to receive Christ as my Savior." It was Maggie's turn to feel shy about her sudden loose tongue. "Anyway," she concluded, "that's when I started attending church again and a Bible study for singles. It's been a lot of new information for me, but I have enjoyed it so much and think I'm learning a lot."

Jim nodded his head in agreement, but didn't say anything. Maggie wondered what he was thinking. She didn't have to wait for long.

"So you're not married?" He asked it so quietly that she had to lean forward to hear him over a burst of laughter from further down their table.

"No. Never have been." She decided she wouldn't know if she didn't ask. "You?"

"I was married. . .for a few years. She had other plans and dreams, neither of which included children. We tried to reach a compromise, but. . ." his voice trailed off. Neither of them spoke for a few long seconds, then Jim broke the silence. "Anyway, she divorced me. She remarried, but died two years later from ovarian cancer."

"I'm sorry," Maggie said again. *Same words, different man.*

"I was sorry to hear it too. Helene really was a neat lady; she just didn't want to try to reconcile our differences." He fumbled with an unused ashtray on the table and did not look up. Maggie felt they had about exhausted their reservoir of conversation. They were, after all, not the kids they used to be and they had not really been close even as teenagers. Still, she had appreciated talking with him beyond jobs and where they now lived.

"I should get back to my table," she said, rising. "It was nice talking with you again, Jim."

"You too, Maggie." He stood as she did. Maggie felt awkward—totally unlike she had felt only minutes ago. Why that was, Maggie wasn't sure. Jim must have sensed the loss of momentum in their conversation too. She noticed now the redness of his ears and he accidentally knocked over his glass of soda when he reached for a pretzel. Maggie jumped back just before the beverage rained down on her shoes.

"I'm sorry, Maggie!" He reached to right the glass and tried mopping up the beverage with some napkins.

"It's okay; missed me by a mile," she said, wiping at her skirt and finding it dry. She helped by adding a few more napkins to the spill on the floor. He came around to her side of the table.

"Sure I didn't get you?" he asked.

"Positive. Let me run and get some paper towels," she offered.

"I'll take care of that. It's not the first time I've knocked something over!" He didn't move, however, and lowered his eyes again to his feet. It was time to say good night, she decided.

"Maybe our next class reunion. . . ?" she asked with a small smile, holding out her hand. Jim did not smile, but rather looked discomfited. He did not see her outstretched hand for a parting good-bye handshake. Instead, he brought his focus from some place on the floor up to Maggie's questioning look.

"Would you see me tomorrow, Maggie?" he blurted out. He ran his tongue nervously across his lower lip, another old habit Maggie suddenly remembered. "That is. . .I thought. . .I thought maybe you would like to go to church with me and then we could go for lunch. But I suppose you've probably made plans with your family," he concluded, his voice heavy with resignation.

Maggie hesitated. What if Dale called her as he said he would? Would she kick herself all the way back to Texas for missing an opportunity to go out with Dale once more? After all, she had to admit she found him titillating to the point of distraction. Should she pass up the chance to go out with a model for a garage mechanic? But since when was one's occupation the measure of a man? Or a man's appearance the most important thing about him? She was so torn! And there stood Jim Gray, now thirty-three, asking her out once again. Waiting for her answer. She made her decision and took a deep breath.

"I think I would like attending your church, Jim. You've piqued my curiosity with your tales of your men's support group for boys and your exotic trips around the world." Her acceptance and smile brought a dramatic brightening to his face.

"You would? That would be great, Maggie! I'll have Randy with me—the young guy I'm mentoring right now. Would that be okay?"

"Of course. I'd like to hear what he thinks of the Triple J program." She smiled and pulled a business card out of her purse and wrote down her parents' address and telephone number. "What time should I expect you?"

"A little before nine." He looked at the card. "I know where this street is. I won't call you unless something comes up. Is that all right?"

"Yes; I'll be ready. See you in the morning," she said, giving him a departing smile. Her reward was a big smile in return. *Even if Dale does call, perhaps I've made the better choice this time.*

"Well?" Cheryl and Marcia asked in unison as she sat back down.

"I'm going to church and lunch with James Gray tomorrow!" she announced.

"Church?" Marcia grimaced. "That's the best you could do?"

"It's a start!" Cheryl said enthusiastically. "Although for the life of me, I can't remember the guy."

Maggie enjoyed her morning with Jim. He seemed much more

relaxed and "in his element" than he had at the reunion. She had to suppress a laugh when she stood between him and Randy during the congregational singing. Both of them were tone deaf, but obviously enjoyed singing anyway. Jim had leaned over afterwards and whispered, "Ran and I make a joyful *noise* to the Lord."

At lunch the three of them laughed a lot. Maggie couldn't believe the transformation. Jim bordered on being what she would call "talkative." He was quick to laugh, and obviously fond of Randy. As they finished their lunch, she excused herself to call home quickly (just to check if Dale had called). He hadn't called. She wasn't seriously disappointed, but her curiosity was satisfied.

She came back to the table slowly. Jim and Randy appeared to be in a serious conversation. She decided to step into the restroom briefly to give them a few more minutes together. She observed them discreetly praying together as she made her way back to their table. They were in open conversation once again as she returned to where they were sitting.

"Ready to go home?" Jim asked before she sat down.

"I think so."

"You don't mind if Jim takes me home first, do you, Maggie?" Randy asked.

"I'm not breaking up your day or any plans you two had?" she asked in return.

"No. I've got to go to work for a few hours. I'm hoping to get a car this summer. Need money for that, don't I, Jim?"

"Big-time," he agreed, picking up the bill and helping Maggie on with her coat. The three of them made their way leisurely to the door, Jim stopping to pay the bill.

After they had dropped Randy at his house, a peeling, unattractive structure among other eyesores in a poor section of the city, Jim's demeanor became serious once again. Maggie remarked on it.

"You seem to really enjoy being with Randy."

"He's quite a kid, isn't he?" he asked, flashing her that shy smile that had disappeared the last few hours. She missed the engaging grin and jocularity she had seen in him while they were with Randy. "I told you I like working with kids. I'm at ease with them."

"That much is obvious." She briefly studied Jim's profile as he drove. "How long have you been in the Triple J program or ministry with him?"

"Probably about two years now. His home life is pretty bad. Alcoholic parents. His dad is abusive if he's been drinking heavily. Both of his parents go on binges and disappear for a couple days or so, leaving Randy to fend for himself. He was referred to our ministry by a guy in the court system who thinks our program is a good one. It was after Randy's first—and only—misdemeanor charge. He and I just clicked from day one."

"Is this how it usually is for you with young guys you mentor through Triple J?"

"No. The first kid I had did well; he's in college now. He calls me once in a while. The second guy was tough. He was a habitual liar. I never knew for sure when he was on the level with me. He did end up going to jail for an assault and battery charge. I've tried to make contact with him, but he's angry and wants nothing to do with me or Jesus or anything worth working for. I just keep praying for him. But I lost a lot of sleep over him too. Not a success story, that's for sure."

There was a pause as Maggie thought about what Jim had just said. What he didn't say spoke more loudly than his words. The sorrow that seemed under the surface or always close at hand in Jim showed in his face as he talked. It was clear he was understating the personal pain he felt for this other young boy.

"I would really like to adopt Randy."

"Why don't you? You guys seem to have such a good relationship."

"Well, for one, I don't think he's ready—yet. And for two, I'm not married. I don't think a child should be in a single parent household if it can be avoided. Of course," he said, turning the corner, "that could change quickly if his stepdad beat him again like he did soon after I met Randy. But he's learned how to stay out of Frank's way if he's been drinking heavily. He calls me and stays with me unless his mom is at home and needs protection from her husband. If Amanda ever leaves and doesn't come back, I won't hesitate to have Randy move in with me. He won't either, I don't think. But for now he's compelled to be there for his mom—when she's there."

Jim pulled into Maggie's parents' driveway and turned off the car. Maggie wondered if she should invite him in, but it seemed awkward. It wasn't her house, after all. Her mother came to the door.

"Maggie! You've got a phone call!" she called as Jim opened Maggie's door.

"Be right there, Mom," she said. "Thank you for such an enjoyable time, Jim. I really did like your church and meeting Randy."

"Are. . .are you busy tonight, Maggie? Would you like to go to a movie or something?"

"Well, why don't you call me later?" she asked. "I want to make sure my folks haven't planned anything with the rest of the family." *And maybe Dale was on the phone now!* She dismissed the thought.

"Oh. Okay. I will."

He walked back around his car and got in. Maggie waved as he pulled away. She ran to the telephone once she was in the house.

"Hello?" she said, hoping she did not sound too eager.

"Hi, Maggie! It's Cheryl."

"Oh, hi, Cheryl." Now she tried to hide the disappointment in her voice.

"Can you come by tonight? I'd like you to see the kids. Besides, we didn't get to talk much last night—you were too popular with the few remaining single men. Which reminds me. . .how did your date go with Jim? Bob? I forgot his name!"

"Jim. It was very pleasant. I had a really nice time with him."

"Good. I looked him up in our senior yearbook, but I barely remember him even looking at what he looked like fifteen years ago."

"He didn't stand out in a crowd then. He was quite shy and kept to himself a lot."

"Did Dale call yet?"

"No. I thought you might be him," Maggie replied, taking off her coat.

"Well, you can't win them all, Mags," Cheryl said, her voice conveying a sympathetic chuckle. "So, what about tonight? If Dale calls you, you could bring him here. Not much fun with two little ones around, but they go to bed early. And you know Harvey; he can talk the leg off anybody!"

"I really would like to see the kids. I'll get over there one way or another. If I bring a man in tow, I'll call you first, okay?"

"Okay. We'll be here all evening. See you later!"

It wasn't five minutes later and the telephone rang again. This time it was Dale.

"Did I wake you up?" he asked after the customary greeting.

"I should hope not!" Maggie answered with a laugh. "It's

almost two o'clock!"

"Really? We didn't roll in until about four; I've done nothing yet today except clean up and drink a gallon of coffee. So, are you free tonight, Maggie?" he asked.

"Sort of. I want to stop over at Cheryl Ewell's and see her kids. She's invited both of us if you wouldn't mind going."

"That would be okay. I've got a place in mind to go later tonight, but we could go there first. Tell me what time to pick you up."

Maggie's anticipation of the evening began to unravel almost as soon as their date started. Dale looked more appealing than he had the night before (if that was possible), and he was as much a gentleman as Maggie could ever remember dating. But they stopped at a store on the way to Cheryl's house. Dale bought fifty dollars' worth of lottery tickets. At the Ewells' house, she overheard Dale telling Harvey about a huge win he had had last year at a racetrack. Cheryl and Harvey found Dale's stories of spending, losing, and winning entertaining. Maggie found it disturbing. When she and Cheryl went to the kitchen to refill beverages and get more munchies, she said as much to Cheryl.

"Don't be ridiculous, Maggie," Cheryl said good-naturedly. "If it wasn't for the lottery our schools would have nothing. And men have been betting on horses forever! I'd do it too if we didn't have to stretch every dime. Dale's lucky to have the money to spend on some fun and frivolity!"

Maggie's trip up to Windsor, Canada, for "a great show and a little gaming" started out to be fun. She had never been to a casino before and found the food and setting to be like nothing she had ever tasted or experienced. Harry, the former classmate who had left with Dale the previous night, was there with his wife and another couple. The six of them shared a lot of laughter and Maggie would have been hard-pressed to remember when she had simply had so many big "belly laughs," as her dad called them. Dale showed her how to play a number of card games and was attentive and complimentary. His gregarious manner and attractive looks quite naturally drew people to him. Maggie caught the interested looks of other women focused on Dale, but he was oblivious to them. In fact, Maggie was almost embarrassed (but certainly thrilled!) that all Dale's attention was on her initially. She won a hundred dollars at one of the games, netting her an affectionate squeeze from Dale.

"Way to go, Magnolia Blossom!" he quipped. And then he spoke more quietly, giving her hand a meaningful squeeze. "I'm so glad you came with me tonight, Maggie. You've made this trip home worth it all. I only came to the reunion hoping to see you again." He touched his hand to her face to brush a stray hair away from her cheek. "It feels so right. Having you here with me." And he held onto her hand or had his arm around her for the next hour or more. Maggie felt protected, happy, excited, and most definitely enamored with the courteous, handsome man beside her.

But after some fun time at the roulette wheels and then the slot machines, Dale had settled in for what he called some "real fun." Maggie joined with him and the other couples in playing at a blackjack table for a while, but she soon tired of it. Especially when she lost the hundred dollars she had won less than two hours ago.

"I'll win it back for you, Maggie," Dale said with a wink. "You just sit here and be my beautiful lady luck." Maggie did sit next to him. She sat for a long time—hour after hour. By midnight she was ready to leave and said something to that effect to Dale.

"In a bit, Maggie. I'm on a roll here," he said.

Harry added his encouragement. "We're all going to be eating well tomorrow! Dale said he'd fly us all up to Mackinac Island for dinner tomorrow if he wins big tonight—and he's winning big!" He and his wife both gave Maggie excited smiles. The excitement was lost on Maggie. She was tired and had had enough of gambling for the day, and very likely for the rest of her life. She wandered aimlessly around the casino for an hour, hoping they would leave soon.

By one-thirty in the morning, Maggie had really had enough. Dale was still playing blackjack; he was so engrossed in the game that he didn't notice a voluptuous blond had sidled in next to him at the table where Maggie had been sitting. Harry and his wife and B.J. and his girlfriend were all busy at different tables and games as well. Maggie excused herself as she wedged herself between the blond and Dale as gently as she could.

"I've got to get going, Dale," she said quietly. He seemed not to hear her, so she repeated herself.

"Already, Maggie?" He signaled the dealer to include him again without looking at Maggie. "Give me another half hour and we'll go, okay?" He didn't wait for her answer as he turned his complete attention back on the game.

At two-thirty, Maggie gave up hope that Dale was going to quit anytime soon. He was down several hundred dollars and she knew from the determined look on his face that he wouldn't get up from the table until he had won it all back and then some. Or lost even more.

"I'm going to have to leave now, Dale," she whispered.

He turned his face to her long enough to meet her eyes with a searching look. "How are you getting home, Maggie?"

"It's all right. I'm a big girl now, Dale." She was kind in her reply, but hurt that he didn't jump up from the table when he saw she was determined to leave.

"Take my car, Maggie. I'll ride home with Harry and Nell. I'll call you tomorrow." He gave her a quick kiss on the cheek, simultaneously reaching into his pocket and pressing his keys into her hand. He turned back to the table. "Deal me in, my man!" he said. "You may be working for me before the night is over!" Everyone at the table laughed, including the dealer. Maggie didn't laugh. She simply walked away, already forgotten by the people huddled at the table.

She gathered her coat and stepped back to take in the imposing, ornate room once more. She had only stayed this long because of Dale. But Dale's attention was neither on her now nor on the room. He was consumed with his activity at the blackjack table. A long sigh escaped her. If anything, the luxurious building was busier and more filled with people now than when they had arrived. The clink of glasses and the background music punctuated the hum of laughter and talking. There were smiles and there were no smiles. People sitting or standing at tables or machines, eagerly or methodically going through practiced motions of "beating the odds" just once. Maggie sighed again and started for the door. This was not the place she wanted to be. And Dale was not the man she wanted to be with.

"It's time to leave here, Lord," she said quietly. A soft voice behind her stopped her.

"Can I take you home, Maggie?"

She reeled in surprise. "Jim! What are you doing here?"

"I can tell you I'm not here to throw good money away," he said somberly. He looked down, but quickly raised his eyes to hers again. There was nothing shy or bashful in the intensity of his direct, but tender, scrutiny of her face.

Maggie knew he understood her and how she felt at that moment. She didn't know how he knew to come here for her, but she would ask him later.

"Wait for me just for a moment, Jim," she said. She went to Harry and gave him Dale's keys.

"Tell Dale I ran into a friend who will be taking me home," she said.

"Oh, okay, Maggie. Maybe we'll see you tomorrow." He dropped the keys into his pocket and turned back to the game.

"Bye, Maggie. Let's do this again sometime!" Nell said.

Maggie gave her a wordless smile, knowing she would not likely see them again. She walked back to Jim, who stood resolutely by the door.

"It's time to go home, Maggie," he said gently. The caress of his loving look shut out the glare and noise around them. She smiled her agreement and together they walked out into the night.

CHAPTER 9

Soul Mates

A heart at peace gives life to the body. . .
—Proverbs 14:30 NIV

I never knew my birth mother."

My new neighbor, Jewel, looked at me in shock.

"I mean," I hastened to correct myself, "I suppose I knew her once, but I've forgotten her completely—her face, her fragrance, her touch. I was almost dead when my Little Mother, Abby, found me and took me in. I owe everything to my adoptive mother, even my life."

My new neighbor has a certain dignity about her. She is clearly older than I and very wise. She thought about my confession for a moment before replying. I was quickly learning that Jewel was a good listener. Probably because she gives careful attention to the speaker (in this case, me) before responding to any question or statement. She is a Jewel; she has a fitting name for someone of her obvious refinement.

"We have one more thing in common then, for I am adopted too," she said with something like awe in her voice. "Would you tell me your story? Then I will tell you mine—though in truth there really is not a great deal to tell." Her eyes were bright with curiosity.

"My tale is brief too," I admitted, feeling somewhat shy to share so personal a thing with someone who was practically a complete stranger to me. Yet I have an uncanny sense that Jewel and I will be lifelong friends from this, our first meeting. Friends like that are rare indeed! I think such friendships are forged in heaven by God Himself before we are but a thought in His eternal mind. But all that is far beyond my capacity to understand!

"My birth mother was not at all like Abby, my Little Mother," I began.

"May I be so bold as to ask you why you call her your 'Little Mother'?" asked Jewel kindly.

"Because she is so little in size! She is not much bigger than I, really. And though she is my mother now, her petite size and her delicate hands sometimes make me feel our roles could easily be reversed, given a change in circumstances."

"I see," said Jewel in her gentle voice. "Please continue with your story then."

"My birth mother did not hover over me, I don't think, as Abby does. If she did, I don't recall it. My first memory is a bleak one. I remember feeling abandoned, cold, and hungry. I was so hungry, Jewel! I can't tell you how much my stomach cried out for food! And the cold! The cold invaded my very bones. I remember thinking, 'After living so short a life, I am going to return to the Good Father who made me. And I shall never be hungry or cold again.' It was a comforting thought on that comfortless dark street."

I shuddered to think of that dark day again. Jewel patiently waited for me to continue.

"The next thing I remember was two warm, gentle hands

lifting me to a warm breast. I wanted to show her I was thankful just for the warm touch, but I could not move for the paralyzing cold and my profound weakness. I felt a hot tear from her eye fall on my head." I paused briefly. "And I knew at that moment I would not die."

Jewel nodded her head in understanding. I smiled in the telling of my story. I had never had a friend to share it with before.

"The next thing I remember is waking up *surrounded* by warmth. Beautiful, heavenly, enveloping warmth! It was wonderful, Jewel! Almost too wonderful to describe! And the gnawing, agonizing hunger pains were gone! For a moment I thought I was with God who is forever praised! But then I saw my Little Mother's eyes dancing with delight to see me opening mine. She squealed with excitement—and almost crushed me in her eager happiness! I think. . ." I thought for a moment. "I think it was the sweetest moment of my life."

"What a wonderful story. And you are happy with this one you call your Little Mother?" Jewel asked.

"So very happy. Sometimes her inexperience as a first-time mother shows. She is too rough—or she is irritatingly gentle!" Jewel laughed with me in understanding. "Then she wants to sleep and I want to play—or vice versa. But all in all I am very happy here in my new home. My old life, quite frankly, is forgotten. I think the cold chilled it out of me, because all I remember is Abby snatching me from certain death."

I couldn't repress a sudden smile as I thought of one item that I had not been so happy about. "I must tell you, Jewel, that the only lament I have is my new name. Of course, for all I know, it may have been my name before my Little Mother saved me. I do not wish to complain, but I do think it's rather. . .odd. Don't you?"

Jewel smiled reflectively in return. "You do not like the name

'Jasper'?" she asked, looking surprised at my confession.

"I have to admit I do not. Your name—Jewel—is so beautiful. And it describes you beautifully too, if you don't mind my saying so."

"How kind of you to say so. Thank you," she said in true humility. "Do you know what 'Jasper' is?" she then asked.

"I must confess I do not!" I said in genuine surprise. "I thought it was a name Abby made up!"

"Not at all. A jasper is a vibrant mineral. It is usually red, yellow, or brown in color. It is a fitting name for you too with your unusual, beautiful coloring. Your Little Mother named you well!"

I had never known that. How remarkable! I was content to think again of the wonder of it all. As far as I'm concerned, Abby is the only mother I have—or will ever have. I was eager to hear Jewel's story now, but her genteel manner was working its influence on me. I waited patiently for her to tell me her story.

"You will be content to stay here always? You are not afraid or suspicious?" she asked.

"Yes. . .and no!" I exclaimed with a happy laugh. "My new home is a wondrous place to live! And I am surrounded by love and care and protection. Mahmii scares me a little bit—but just a little bit. She has a big voice, which often startles me. She treats me just as tenderly as my Abby does—perhaps even more so—just not as often. Abby is very generous with her hugs and kisses. I don't believe I will ever tire of them."

"I understand completely," replied Jewel. Again I waited for her to continue, which she now did.

"My story is similar to yours in that I am a fortunate orphan too. But I know what happened to my birth mother." Jewel looked so very sad that I could almost feel her pain in my own heart. (I am learning that deepening friendships are not all joy and laughter. Sometimes the pain of others takes up residence in our own hearts.)

"My birth mother was killed by a speeding automobile."

"No!" I gasped. *What a horrible thing!*

"It was a horrible thing," she said, echoing my very thought. "My younger brother had crossed the street in direct disobedience to her repeated warnings to both of us. One minute he and I were playing happily in the backyard and the next, he was gone. I did not know where he had gone! Mother came outside, frantic to see he was not with me. I followed her as she went around to the front yard. There, across the street, sat Tommy crying." Jewel stopped for a moment, the memory a grievous one for her. "I think in her haste my mother forgot her own rules about watching for automobiles. She just ran for Tommy and. . . and then she was gone. It happened so quickly that Tommy and I could do nothing but stare at each other from across the street."

"How awful for both of you," I said, meaning it. I preferred having no memory of my birth mother to having such a painful one as Jewel's! How did she live with the ache of it? "I am so sorry," I said. What else is there to say?

"It was awful, but that is how Belinda came into our lives. She stepped in, scooped us up into her loving arms, and took us in from that very day. It all happened some time back. I was about the age you are now. I did not and do not understand the legalities of our adoption, but neither do I care. Like you, I am grateful our great God provided a home for us—for both of us to stay together!"

"Does Tommy still live with you and Belinda?" I asked.

"Yes, but he has to be watched constantly or he is forever straying. He is older now, so I suppose that's to be expected. Belinda seems quite resigned to it."

"Do you ever call Belinda your mother?" I asked, since

Jewel had her memories of her natural mother.

"I think of her that way, but no, I do not refer to her as such usually. But I too love her as you love Abby." She stretched once, very regally, and rose to go back inside her house.

"It has been delightful getting to know you, Jasper. I look forward to seeing you again in the morning. I know where we can get an excellent breakfast!"

"It's been a pleasure for me too, Jewel. I think I hear my Little Mother calling me, so I must run home. Thank you for the invitation for breakfast! I'll look for you bright and early!"

We part for the time being, my new friend and I. I hear Abby calling me as I come closer to home.

Her entire face glows with her big, bright smile as I round the gate. "Jasper! There you are! I've been calling and calling for you!"

She eagerly picks me up and I see Mahmii coming behind her. I should not have been gone for so long. I welcome both my Little Mother's overzealous squeeze as well as Mahmii's approving smile and pat on my head.

"She's home, Mommy! Jasper heard me calling and came running home!"

"So she has, Abby darling. Let's go in and reward her with her favorite snack and brush her beautiful fur. Your daddy will soon be here to meet your new kitten for the first time."

Now I remember what I forgot.

I meant to ask wise Jewel who or what a Dahdii is!

CHAPTER 10

Made for Each Other

Delight yourself in the LORD and
he will give you the desires of your heart.
—Psalm 37:4 NIV

I just know you will enjoy meeting my niece, Pastor!" Mrs. Welsh crooned. She shook his hand as vigorously as she shook out her dust cloth. Pastor Gabe Hollowell was sure his arm would be disconnected from his shoulder. How could such a tiny old lady be so strong? He put on a big smile.

"I'm sure I will too, Mrs. Welsh. Thank you for the dinner invitation." He waved to the church's senior pastor across the foyer who was either trying to rescue him from Mrs. Welsh or who was, in fact, trying to hale him to his side. Gabe excused himself quickly and walked over to Pastor Wilson Carter. Gabe himself had come on staff as minister of music just four months ago. It was almost one o'clock this Sunday afternoon. Most of the two thousand people who filled the sanctuary earlier had left. Wilson excused himself from the couple with whom he had been talking.

"I need you to step into my office for a minute, Gabriel,"

the elderly man said, steering Gabe quickly away from any of the other late-departing congregation. "We must have received this fax late last night. It wasn't here when I left yesterday afternoon." He unlocked the door and they entered his small office. Gabe was still impressed by the austerity of this man with whom he served on staff. The senior pastor of a large, growing church was content with—had insisted upon, he had heard—the smallest office in the building when he had come to Crossgates himself fifteen years ago.

"Big offices can intimidate people who have big problems," he had told Gabe when Gabe had been a candidate for the position of minister of music. "Jay needs the bigger office for those groups of kids he's always meeting with. And when his wife and their kids come in to take their daddy out to lunch, he needs it all the more!" He had laughed then, making a reference to their youth pastor who had a family of five children and one more on the way. He had gone on to tell Gabe that he thought people were more likely to be up front with him if they weren't distracted by shelves of Greek and Hebrew lexicons interspersed with books on counseling and sermonizing. So, his office consisted of four chairs; a dark mahogany desk; the standard office fare of computer, telephone, and the like; and a large window that looked out over the small stretch of land that bordered on the adjacent university's arboretum. The senior pastor seldom closed the draperies, giving the office the feel of a cozy study. A worn Bible was on the desk atop a daily planner. A large picture on one wall was of his grandchildren. Gabe reflected how the office had had a calming effect on him when he had first come to Crossgates Church. The office was an extension of Pastor Carter himself: humble, quiet, soothing—the tender side of a man whom Gabe had grown to admire very quickly.

"Here it is!" Wilson announced after shuffling through some

papers. "There's been a change for our missions conference next week. The national office said that Geri Haller won't be able to make it; she broke her leg and won't be traveling for a while. They've suggested we have. . .um. . .her name is. . ." He scanned the paper quickly. "MaryEllen Nee." He handed the sheet to Gabe while he continued to talk.

"I don't know Miss Nee," he said. "She's a new missionary with our denomination and has been serving in Guinea, West Africa. They weren't able to send a photo or anything since she has only been back from overseas a month. She was willing to come on short notice since she will be moving here to pick up some classes at the university. We might get more information about her or from her during the week, I hope."

He continued while Gabe looked over the fax. "The reason I called this to your attention, Gabe, is that she is a musician. Perhaps you'd like to contact her about what she plans to do musically when she's here. The number where you can reach her is there on the fax."

"Thanks, Wils, I'll do that. By the time you come back on Thursday, I should have some information for you. The Missions Committee has everything else taken care of, right?"

"Yes—as long as we don't get any other last-minute changes! They're making arrangements for the missionaries to be picked up at the airport. Sorry to spring this on you today, but Louise and I are catching a plane ourselves in a few hours and I wanted to make sure you got this."

They left his office and hadn't walked five steps when one of the members of the church pulled Pastor Carter away. Gabe made his way back to his own office to lock up and noticed he had messages on his voice mail. He set aside the fax as the recorder started.

"Pastor Hollowell, this is Marcy. I won't be able to sing

tonight. I've got a house full of sick kids. Sorry to leave you in the lurch. I owe you one. . ." *Great,* he thought. Now he'd have to find somebody else to sing tonight. The machine continued. "Gabe? George here. I can't do the sound tonight. Rusty's team won yesterday and they play again tonight. Sorry!" *Double great,* he groaned. I suppose the pianist won't be able to make it either. . . .

"Gabe? This is Wendy." Gabe looked at the telephone in shock. A voice from the past—he sat down before he fell down. The recorder continued. "It's been a long time, I know. I have a proposition for you. Call me. . . ." She gave a number and hung up.

Gabe wrote down the number and pushed the "delete" button. He had never expected to hear from Wendy again. How had she found him? Called his folks? Called his former college roommate? He hadn't talked to her in six. . .maybe eight years! He had thought about her occasionally. Her face or her laughter would come unbidden at the strangest times and in the most unsettling ways. He didn't know what to make of this call.

Wendy had been a part of the old Gabe Hollowell—the reckless goof-off who had almost blown his full ride at college. He had spent more time having fun than practicing at the piano or vocalizing during his first two years of undergraduate school. Fortunately for him, his roommate persuaded Gabe to join him for a small Bible study. From that study Gabe had become a believer in Jesus Christ. He had always known *about* Christ, but only in the same way he knew *about* Mozart or Bach or Einstein. That Bible study had been the beginning of all that was dear to him now, but it also marked the end of some things that were dear to him then. Like his relationship with Wendy.

They had been so alike, so. . .meant for each other. She was in Performance Voice and was determined to make it big in show business. She did have an incredible voice. She had done major musical roles in Los Angeles, where they both went to school. He knew she had had small parts in Broadway productions and had recently had a major part in a movie. It looked like that would take her where she wanted to go. Her name was becoming known and she had had some popular hits. He was glad for her.

But his commitment to Jesus Christ was something she did not understand. Something she *would* not understand. At first she humored him about it. Then she indulged him his new-found faith. Then she became teasing, then angry. Finally she became tolerant of his "religious thing," as she called it. But when Gabe told her of his change of plans regarding his future career, that he planned to go into full-time music ministry, her tolerance came to an abrupt end.

"Why would you do that, Gabe?" she had asked, incredulous. "You are too talented to go that route! You can make it big in entertainment! We *both* can—especially as a team!"

She had cried, had begged, had done everything she could to dissuade him from his choice. But he had already seen enough of the venomous competition, the "performance at any price" mind-set, the demanding constraints of professional entertainment—and the dark lures that surrounded it all—that he had opted out for good by the time he had completed his bachelor's degree. His master's work only strengthened his resolve. Wendy pursued her dream and he, his. Their paths separated and he, for one, did not look back. But sometimes longing for her brought flashbacks of tender times and the inevitable "what if. . .?" Could they have stayed together? Made a go of it? He didn't think so then. Now he found himself wondering if it could have been. . . if it could yet be.

Wendy had been his first love. Once he had made an all-out

commitment to Jesus Christ, however, he knew they could not "be a team" professionally or intimately. Their commitments and goals were worlds apart. She grew frustrated with his "God talk" and he grew dismayed over her resistance to discuss his new-found faith. They began drifting apart: emotionally, philosophically, and socially. Finally, they had mutually walked away from each other. But maybe—he snapped the lid shut on his brief case—maybe she had changed. Maybe the glitter had lost its allure for her. Maybe. . .

"Are we far away in never-never land?" The voice brought him back to reality.

"Hey, Donna! I didn't hear you." *And I was in never-never-ever-again land,* he thought. He rose to leave.

"I thought the choir number went well today, didn't you?" The self-appointed organizer of All Things Pertinent to the Music Ministry picked up his copy of the song the choir had sung earlier and dropped it into the filer she carried.

"Yes, I did. Thanks for grabbing that. It would have been lost by Wednesday. I appreciate your organizational skills, Donna. Keeps things around here from total chaos."

"You music people are all alike," she said, her harsh tone covering what he knew to be a spirit of service. "Great for the *ministry* of the church, but useless when it comes to the every-day *business* of the church. Are you set for lunch? Not doing that fast-food route, are you?"

"No," he said, smiling. "I've got some leftover chicken casse-role and fruit to eat before I roll back in for tonight's service. How about doing a special number for us tonight? Marcy had to cancel."

"A solo? Hah! They'd throw me out of the church and you'd lose your job! No thanks!" She exited his office and he followed her out the door.

"How about sound? The sound man can't make it either."

"You looking to get fired or something?" she asked, stuffing the folder into its proper spot.

"No, but I can't do both. Thought you might be willing to help me out of a jam," he replied.

"I'll file your music, I'll clean up your coffee machine, I'll even dust the piano. But I won't do solo and I won't do sound and I won't preach." She closed the door with an authoritative bang and then turned to give him a smiling reminder. "See you tonight, Gabriel. Get home to your chicken and to your telephone. Sunday's not your day off!"

Monday was not Gabe's day off either. Things had worked out well for the Sunday night service, especially with the rain canceling Rusty Schuster's game. But Monday had begun early with Gabe going to the hospital to pray with one of the church's families who had a medical emergency. With the senior pastor gone, the youth pastor out of the office for his day off, and the associate pastor meeting with other local pastors across town, Gabe had enough to do trying to cover for everyone.

Even the secretaries were on the brink of screaming. A water pipe broke and then the copy machine decided to spew ink all over the office carpeting. One of the kids (presumably it had not been an adult) had spent a good deal of time locking all the restroom stalls from the inside, which meant Gabe had to crawl under each door to unlock them. Usually that type of thing was a custodial headache, but the one custodian who was at the church on this particular Monday had a bad back. So the bothersome task had fallen to Gabe. And always at the back of his mind was the call from Wendy. By four o'clock Gabe was ready to run for his apartment and disconnect his telephone before another emergency hit. But his telephone was ringing when he walked in.

"Hello, Pastor Holloway?"

"This is Gabe Hollowell," he answered, praying he wouldn't have to go back across town to the hospital.

"This is MaryEllen Nee. I'll be at Crosswise next week. . . ?"

"Crossgates," he corrected. He was trying to think who Mary Ellen Nee was. The missionary. That's who it was. He pulled off his shoes and loosened his tie. Her enunciation was precise, but she had a voice that sounded like gravel. It grated on his already-taut nerves. "Yes, Miss Nee. What can I do for you?"

"I am so sorry to call you at your home," she said. "But I had some questions and one of the secretaries at your church gave me your home telephone number. Do you have a few minutes?"

"Sure."

He continued through his apartment to change clothes. He resisted dropping onto the bed, afraid he wouldn't get up again if he did. The woman on the other end of the telephone sounded about one hundred years old. In his brief experience as a minister of music, he decided that was about the going age of most foreign missionaries. He doubted she was a vocalist—not with a voice like that! She must be some kind of instrumentalist. Pastor Carter had said she was some kind of musician. He had never had time to think about the fax at work today, let alone do any calling about it.

"My flight schedule was changed and I will be coming in Friday evening instead of Saturday. Will that be a problem?" she asked.

"I don't think so. One of the ladies at the church was going to pick you up. If she can't make it, we'll make arrangements with someone else. Just give me the flight information and we'll take care of everything. We received your fax. You're a musician?" he asked, continuing to change into his biking attire.

"A cellist. I can play a few other instruments also." She asked questions about the week of services and who the other mission- ary speaker would be. For his part, Gabe asked her about doing some special instrumental numbers, including a duet or two with him. They agreed on a few numbers to do together and she also offered to play with the church orchestra. They ended their conversation with plans to rehearse together on Saturday. Gabe was eager to get off the telephone and get on his bicycle. He bid the gravelly voice a good-bye and hung up.

Before his telephone could ring again—or he could think about calling Wendy back—he grabbed his helmet and biking shoes, and went out to make his regular twenty-five-mile cycling circuit. He would deal with calling Wendy when he got back— *if* he called her. He needed to work the kinks out of his back and the ache out of his head from his day at work. Sometimes he pri- vately labeled the music ministry "the music misery." Today had been no exception, and there'd been far more misery than music.

"Wendy. This is Gabe."

Gabe sat at his kitchen table in his jeans and T-shirt, his fingers drumming a slow beat on the tabletop. He didn't know what to expect and not knowing what to expect made him uncomfortable. His long bike trek had done nothing to allevi- ate his apprehension about this telephone call.

"Gabe! It's wonderful hearing your voice again! Thank you for calling back. I'm sure you're wondering why I called. I got your number at work—is it okay to call a church your 'work'? —from Karl. He said to be sure and tell you 'hi' and to E-mail him or give him a call. Says he hasn't talked to you since you relocated to Michigan." Her words came out in a disconnected staccato.

"I've been pretty busy, but that's no excuse." He paused. *Let's get to the point here,* he thought, still ill at ease. "So, how are you, Wendy? It looks like your career is really starting to take off."

"Yes, it is and it's wonderful! But it can be exhausting too. Sometimes I wonder if my vocal cords will last another minute!" Her light laughter sounded good to his ears. "So how is it—being a preacher?"

"Well, I'm not a preacher, Wendy. I'm a minister of music. I only preach as a pinch hitter. If all the other staff fall sick or are gone, I'll preach, but otherwise the music aspect is a full-time job and then some."

"Do you like it?" she asked.

That's the Wendy I used to know. Doesn't mince words.

"Yes, I do. I can't think of anything else I'd rather do," he said honestly. She was silent for a few seconds. He finished his glass of water and walked to his living room.

"Well, I'm sure you're wondering why I called," she said finally, her voice all business. "I'm supposed to do a benefit performance there in Michigan in two weeks. I think the city is just a couple hours from where you live. I was wondering if you could play a couple numbers for me. I do have a backup group who travels with me, but I thought it would be a nice chance for us to get together again and get you more exposure to people other than those at your church. How about it? It would be gratis—it *is* a benefit performance, but I would be willing to pay you for your time."

"I'm flattered that you would consider having me play for you. But I don't know, Wendy. I've got a really busy week coming up. Maybe we could just get together and. . ."

But Wendy would have nothing of getting together without performing together. She wouldn't take "no" for an answer, promised to send him the music overnight, and arranged for all of one rehearsal the day of the benefit. One rehearsal and one day. That was all he would see her. Maybe it would be enough. Maybe it wouldn't be enough at all. The conversation left him feeling drained, disagreeable, and out of sorts. If anything had changed about Wendy, it was her persistence. She had not only honed her skill at getting what she wanted; she had perfected it. He moodily reached for his daily calendar and penciled in the concert.

By the time Saturday arrived, Gabe was ready to leave the ministry and the country. Two funerals during the week demanded he be at church to take care of the sound system and music for both services. The music he had been expecting for the final day of their missions conference was on back order; it would not be there in time for the closing service. The CD player in the sound booth of the sanctuary had to be repaired. The piano tuner, who came as scheduled, insisted he had to tell Gabe every little thing he did to all six of the pianos in the facility. Donna was sick and he had to take care of all those organizational things she had told him he was no good at. To his chagrin he learned she was right. He couldn't find anything and Wednesday's choir rehearsal was a jumble of trying to locate more copies of music, tracking down a CD he had misplaced, and silencing the sopranos' nonstop talking and giggling.

To top it all off, he'd had an inner tube blow out while biking on Thursday. That netted him a scraped arm, a banged-up knee, and gravel embedded in his right calf. He had forgotten to replace tubes and cartridges from his last mishap and had ended up hobbling back towards his apartment for a mile or two before some Good Samaritan picked him up. And always at the corner of his consciousness were the benefit concert and the prospect of seeing Wendy again. He had begun losing sleep over the whole thing, in spite of praying about it daily. He'd even dreamed Wendy had come to his church and pulled him off the platform while he was directing a choir number! He had to take two aspirin as soon as he woke that morning.

Now he was waiting for the precocious Miss Nee to hobble into the sanctuary for a brief rehearsal with him. He was practicing the two numbers he would be doing with Wendy, once again sorry he had agreed to do the benefit. He didn't feel emotionally ready to tackle a performance with Wendy. He would be playing with a professional band in front of a bunch of rich stuffed shirts who were trying to save rain forests, whales, or egrets. He couldn't even remember what the concert was for! He quietly sang the melancholy song he played. It matched his dark mood.

"Pastor Holloway?"

Gabe stopped at the sound of the familiar rasping voice. He stood and quickly took in the missionary with whom he had communicated a half dozen times in the past week. She was not elderly; she was not wrinkled. In fact, nothing in her appearance matched her voice. Her luminous dark eyes sparkled with a cautionary greeting. She had what he thought must be bad scarring from a burn. It started along the right side of her face and ran down the right side of her neck. Although it pulled her mouth slightly down and over, there was something invitingly winsome about her. Her loose-fitting blouse and jeans contrasted with the mental picture he had drawn of her in a poorly fitting polyester suit and squat black shoes. She walked toward him, set down her cello, and extended her hand. He stood up from the piano bench and shook her offered hand, which was also scarred.

"It's Gabe, remember? Gabe Hollowell."

"Please, call me Ellie," she said. "I am sorry to keep getting your name wrong. It is one of my worst flaws. Speaking three languages leaves my brain muddied!"

Muddled, he smiled to himself, but kept his silence. He had no room to talk; he did well to speak just one language.

"What is that you were playing when I walked in?" she asked. "I didn't recognize the melody, although I must say it is beautiful!" She began getting her cello out of its case.

"It's called 'Wishing.' It's a fairly new popular song. Here, let me get you a chair. . ." He positioned a chair adjacent to the piano and struck a cord as she tightened her bow string.

"Something for here at church?" she asked, tuning up with him between words.

"No. I'm playing for a friend next Saturday at a benefit concert." He handed her copies of the music they would be doing at the church and quickly changed the subject. "These are the songs we talked about doing. Have you seen these arrangements before?"

"No, so let's take it slowly to begin."

For the next hour the two of them were heavily engrossed in playing, making adjustments on the musical score, playing some more, and drafting more changes. Ellie was quick to laugh at her own mistakes. She told him she hadn't played her cello much in recent weeks. She was too busy becoming acclimated to American culture once again. Her talent was unmistakable, however, and Gabe found she was quick to make minor changes in the musical score that improved the songs. A few times he lost his place; it was easy to become distracted by her accomplished mastery of the cello. They didn't have a cellist in their church orchestra. Her addition to the orchestra would be an extra bonus.

MaryEllen was witty, talented, and outspoken. He learned all that in short order. He had expected to leave as soon as they finished practicing. But he found her so refreshing to his weariness that he lingered at the piano, singing and playing a couple of songs while she improvised on the cello. Thoughts of his upcoming concert with Wendy were pushed to the background, bringing welcome relief to the mental turmoil of his last few days.

"Would you mind doing one or two numbers like this during the week if needed?" he asked.

"Not at all. We missionaries are a bold lot, you know! We grow accustomed very quickly to improvisation and adaptation. Sometimes that is good. Sometimes it is not. We expect the same of others who are more used to an orderly, comfortable, structured way of life." He nodded in agreement. Sometimes his church choir did not like last-minute changes he threw at them. And he himself was disliking the disorder Wendy's call had brought into his daily routine.

"If you like, you can leave your cello behind the stage here and it will be safe," he said. "Do you need a ride back to Donna's house?"

"No. Her house is within walking distance without my cello—thank you—if I don't get lost. Besides, I could use a little exercise."

"Same here. Let me walk you back there. I can come back here for my car." They left the sanctuary and Gabe turned out the lights and set the alarm system as they stepped out into the unseasonably warm November sunshine.

"I am so glad it is warm. Donna tells me that it is usually much colder here this time of year. I must confess I am much more used to my African heat and humidity."

"Pastor Carter tells me you've only been a missionary for the last four years, but that your parents were missionaries too."

"Yes. I grew up in Kenya. My father is of Chinese decent; he was the first-generation American in his family. My parents are still there in Kenya with my two youngest brothers. I have another brother in college in Florida. In fact, he will be driving up next week to bring the rest of my things. I have a furnished apartment that I will be moving into next week. It is a long story how I came to have it, but Donna has offered to help me clean it and set up housekeeping. It will be a new experience for me! What few years I have spent in the U.S. were in my college dormitory. I am so fortunate to be staying with Donna! We were friends from our first 'hello.' Although she is much older than I, we are soul mates in many ways! And she is making me feel right at home already! She told me she sings in your choir here."

She dropped her eyes and kicked a stone off the sidewalk. "I am talking too much. Have you been here at. . .Crossgates long?" she asked, her rasping voice quieter.

"Actually, no; just a few months. I did a short stint in youth ministry in California before moving here. Youth ministry wasn't my thing, but I had bills to pay and a big church out there offered me a temporary position until they could get the man they wanted and I could get the job I wanted. It turned out to be an equitable arrangement. And I must say I enjoyed it too. It was a great learning experience and the kids I worked with were the best."

She asked him more questions about the church, the music ministry, and the university where she would begin taking classes in January. He walked her up to Donna's door. His most faithful alto and office organizer met them as they stepped up to the porch.

"Hi, Gabe. Care to come in and join Ellie and me for a cup of coffee?"

"No, thanks, Donna. Are you feeling better?"

"Yes. It was just one of those twenty-four-hour bugs. I was glad to recover in time for Ellie's arrival. Sure you won't join us?" she asked.

"Yes. Thanks just the same. See you both in the morning!"

Gabe turned around and sauntered back to the church, unaware of Ellie's penetrating gaze following him before she closed the door.

Sunday was full and busy for Gabe, who had little time to eat, let alone think about or practice for the benefit concert. He found both Ellie and their other guest missionary to be compelling speakers. The music went better than he thought it would. Even the Sunday night service flowed nicely. Gabe still marveled at how God always orchestrated details so wonderfully. Had he or Pastor Carter planned every little element of the service, it could not have been better. As the week progressed, his apprehension about the benefit concert with Wendy dissipated. It wasn't that he thought about it and no longer worried; he simply didn't have time to think about it. When he wasn't busy setting up microphones or video equipment, he was practicing music with Ellie, the church praise team, or some other musicians. By Thursday evening, he gladly joined a group Donna had invited to her house for some light refreshments. The missions conference had been great, but a very tired Gabe was glad it was over.

He loosened his tie, grateful to sit and relax. Ellie came and sat near him.

"Thank you for all your hard work this week, Gabe. The music added so much to the entire tone of the services."

"Thank you, Ellie. It's not every day we get to have a missionary with us who can play an instrument as well as she can preach! Do you think you'll be staying at Crossgates?"

"Oh, yes. I think it will easily be my USA home church. It's unlikely I'll be able to return to my beloved Africa, so this is all going to be a new adventure for me. I'm still trying to get used to all the changes and the huge stores again! Grocery stores are always an overwhelming cultural hurdle after living in simplicity for so long. I find myself standing agape when I first enter one. So many choices! It really is hard to get used to after being away for so long."

"You and Les have given us an education this week! I never knew how hard it might be to get used to the U.S. after so many years away from it. I think it would be harder to get used to a place like Guinea than Michigan!"

"Not at all. The pace here, the choices for everything from food to entertainment—it's all quite overwhelming for a while." She scratched the deep scar on her neck and sipped her beverage.

"Tonight you talked about the fire you were in as a child. Do you still have pain from the damage to your skin and vocal cords?" he asked.

"Not now. The grafting and all was excruciatingly painful, but God, as always, showed Himself faithful to me. Another part of the healing was to my mind. I was angry with God for a long time because of my disfigurement and the damage to my voice. But I can still talk and have almost no physical limitations, so I cannot complain. God is good to heal our past pains, wouldn't you agree?" she asked.

"Yes," Gabe answered, but he felt less confident about that as Saturday loomed closer. He had dreaded seeing Wendy again. And he couldn't wait to see her again. The pain he experienced years ago in separating himself from her—and her from him—had returned somehow. The prospect of seeing her again, of talking with her again, had given him cause to do some soul-searching. Would he be able to walk away from her again? It was difficult enough the first time. They were both older now. Had the years softened both of them that each might be willing to meet the other halfway? Now that life had fallen into a more predictable routine, he wasn't sure he wasn't somewhat enticed by the possibility of. . .

"Gabe?"

He realized he had missed something Ellie said. "I'm sorry, Ellie. What did you say?"

"I asked if you're ready for that benefit concert you told me about."

"I. . .uh. . .yes, I think so. I'm a little intimidated by it. The friend who called me—Wendy is her name—is pretty confident we can pull this off. I'm not sure I won't just go blank! She's a pro now and has a professional group that tours with her. To be frank, I'm sorry I agreed to do it. Obviously," he said, smiling with some embarrassment, "it's caused me no small amount of distraction."

"Her name is Wendy? Wendy what?" Ellie asked.

"You might know her by her professional name: Wesli Forano."

"No, I don't think I've heard of her. But remember I've only been back in the U.S. for a little over a month. I'm still trying to catch up with the national news! Entertainment news has not been a priority for me." She paused and Gabe self-consciously brushed some imaginary lint from his slacks. He didn't like thinking about Wendy, let alone talking about her.

"She is very talented?" Ellie asked.

"Very talented," he answered with emphasis.

"Very beautiful?"

Gabe remembered Wendy's silken blond hair, her alabaster skin, her. . .he stopped himself. *Lord, help me keep my perspective here,* he prayed before answering Ellie. She regarded him with open curiosity.

"Oh yes. Very beautiful too. That's why she is where she is: a rising star who's attracted the attention of movie producers as well as Broadway bigwigs. Believe me, by this time next year she'll be a big draw in the entertainment industry. Which is what she always wanted." *And what she'll always want.*

"Is she or was she very special to you?" Ellie asked. Before he could answer she raised her scarred hand and waved off his response. "I am prying. Forgive me." She stopped, took a breath, and smiled sweetly. "What are the songs you will be playing for her during this program?"

Gabe was glad for the safer question. "The one you heard me playing last week,'Wishing,' and another popular show tune entitled 'Far From You.' " A sudden idea came into Gabe's head uninvited. "Would you like to go with me? It's a bit of a drive and I could use the company to settle my nerves." *Why did I just do that?* he asked himself.

"How kind of you to ask, Gabe! Would it be permissible for me to go?"

"Sure!" he said, not knowing if it would be or not. There was no retracting his invitation now. "You could do some shopping there in Detroit if you wanted. It's a much larger city than our town here."

"No shopping, please!" Ellie laughed. "Donna has had me in every shop in every town within a ninety-mile radius of here! I am 'shopped out.' " She regarded him with a look he couldn't quite read. She dropped her eyes briefly, then looked up again with a smile.

"I would like to go. I need to become familiar with American popular music or my ignorance will convince my fellow students and professors that I just came from another planet and not another country! Thank you. Tell me the time, what I should wear (I've never been to a benefit concert before), and I'll be happy to accompany you."

Late Saturday afternoon Gabe and Ellie arrived in Detroit. Wendy's manager, a man with a deep baritone voice, had called

Gabe to give him directions to the hotel where they would meet them. He instructed Gabe to "dress comfortably" but to bring a tuxedo. Gabe didn't own a tuxedo, but had anticipated needing one and so was prepared. He called Ellie and told her to bring a dressy change of clothes.

A luxurious suite was awaiting them, which made Gabe more nervous and Ellie feel awkward. He told himself again he should have never invited Ellie along. What had he been thinking? But just when he began to apologize to Ellie for this unforeseen development, she shocked him with a long whistle.

"*This* is unbelievable!" she said, her hand touching the velvety surface of one of the room's love seats. "Will these people have enough money left over for their cause when they have finished paying the bill for your locker room?" He looked at her in surprise and they both burst out laughing.

Within minutes Ellie was cordially shown to an adjacent room, "compliments of Miss Forano," the young, bashful hotel employee told her. Both Gabe and Ellie were relieved to have separate rooms—even if the rooms were only for freshening up. Ellie stayed in her room while Gabe went to rehearse with Wendy.

He was picked up at the door by a man in a limo and ushered to the performance hall a few blocks away. None of this did anything to settle Gabe's nerves and he hoped Ellie was praying for him as he had asked her to do. He could not remember being this nervous. Ever.

"Gabe!"

Wendy rushed to him as he entered the building. She was even more beautiful than Gabe remembered. Her fragrance took him back to the lilies of the valley they used to sit beside in their carefree, dreamy days. She barely touched her cheek to his and quickly grabbed his hand.

"Come and meet my crew," she said, pulling him towards the grand piano that gleamed under penetratingly bright overhead lights.

She introduced him with giddy abandon to a mixed assortment of musicians, scarcely giving him time to say "hello" to any of them. It was just as well. Gabe could not think beyond the touch of her hand in his. The aura of sparkle and vivaciousness that surrounded her made the overhead lights appear dim in comparison.

"And this," she said, turning Gabe to face a man who regarded him with little emotion, "is my manager, Len Forester." The handsome man extended his hand.

"Nice to meet you, Hollowell. Wesli has told me a lot about you." His grip was tight; so was his smile. It went no higher than his upper teeth. Gabe noticed the way he looked at Wendy. Protectively. Possessively. Gabe suspected there was more to their relationship than business.

"Get to it, folks. Run through these numbers with Mr. Hollowell here and then we can break before tonight's show. See you after the performance, Hollowell." Len Forester turned to Wendy and said quietly, "See you at the hotel, Wes." Gabe didn't miss the look that passed between them and, for all the years and differences that separated him from Wendy, he wasn't sure it didn't hurt.

"Let's do 'Wishing' first, okay, Gabe?" Wendy asked, not waiting for him to answer. He sat at the piano and helped the band tune their instruments. That was the closest he got to Wendy before the performance. And he hadn't been given a chance to speak one word to her. Nor did he after they finished rehearsing; she was whisked away by the band director. Gabe received a distracted smile and wave from Wendy, who was busily engaged in conversation with the musician. Unceremoniously,

Gabe was taken back to the hotel.

"How did it go?"

After a shower, a change of clothes into the rented tuxedo, and no little amount of time in prayer, Gabe stood to meet a beautifully dressed MaryEllen Nee in the hotel lobby. She wore a gown of gently shimmering violet. The dress had a high neckline and long sleeves that hid most of her scarring. Except for the disfigurement of the right side of her face, she looked stunning to him.

"Wow! You look great, Ellie!"

"Am I overdressed? Donna borrowed this dress for me from someone—she said it would be just right for something like this." Her large eyes looked to him for assurance. "I feel most uncomfortable," she said in a lower tone.

"You look stunning. You'll fit right in with whoever is there." He helped her on with her coat, noting her diminutive size and the gleam of her coal-black hair under the lobby lights. He was suddenly conscious of Ellie as an attractive, single young woman. It was obvious she was ill at ease and for the first time it struck him how Wendy might read Ellie's presence here with him. What in the world had he been thinking?

"You didn't answer my question, Gabe. How did the rehearsal go?" she asked, intruding upon his thoughts. He pushed the diversion of her closeness away and ran his finger around his neck, pushing at the collar of the stiff shirt.

"Fine," he answered. She turned back to straighten his tie, lifting her eyes to read in his face what he didn't say. *Is she reading my mind?* he wondered. Her eyes held his for just a moment.

"It didn't really now, did it? You don't seem any the less agitated than earlier."

Suddenly, Ellie too seemed to be conscious of her physical closeness to Gabe. She quickly dropped her hands from his tie, her eyes from his, and took a step backwards. "I am sorry. I am prying again."

"No, it's okay, really." He took a deep breath and looked to the lobby entrance before answering. "The music went fine. It has been a long time since I sat in the same room, listening to Wendy sing. It brought back a flood of memories I wasn't quite prepared for. Plus. . ." he hesitated.

"Plus?" she prompted.

"Plus I really wasn't even given a chance to talk with her. It was all business. Show business." He looked away from Ellie's tender expression before he added. "I'm just some local talent she's giving an 'opportunity' to for who knows what reason." He was angry with himself that he had read things into their telephone conversation that were not there. His proximity to Wendy had changed for today. His distance from her had not. He saw the limousine pull up to the door of the hotel. He gestured to the door and took Ellie's arm. "Our coach is here, Cinderella. Let's go to the ball."

The concert went extremely well. The two numbers that Gabe had performed with Wendy were especially well received, he thought. Ellie had been seated at a table with the people who had coordinated the event. Gabe had been whisked away from the table before the appetizer had been served to receive last-minute instructions from Wendy's manager and the band director. They also "layered him" with makeup that he went to extremes to remove as quickly as he could when he finished his segment of the program.

He did not see Wendy until she was performing onstage; he watched from the wings until it was time for him to play.

He accompanied her, made his bows, and was ushered to a rear table to hear the rest of Wendy's performance soon after their two numbers together. He had to admit he enjoyed it; her voice was remarkable, her talent unmistakable, her delivery unbeatable. She was a professional in every sense of the word. Her performance left the audience, himself included, on their feet in zealous applause. He had struggled to make his way back to Ellie, as people stopped him to shake his hand and laud his part in the concert.

He was surprised to find Ellie looking like she had been crying when he finally managed to get to her table. They had no time to talk, however, for one of Wendy's troupe very quickly took them backstage. Gabe felt awkward as he and Ellie were essentially ignored in all the hubbub around Wendy. He noticed Ellie dabbing a tissue to her eyes, moistening her lips nervously, and lifting her chin in what he could only construe as a habit of tackling a new situation. She squared her small shoulders and stood to her full height—which wasn't much. He smiled to himself. Obviously, she wasn't about to let this new American experience intimidate her into shrinking passivity.

"You were wonderful!" Wendy gushed, suddenly up against him and once again, just barely touching her cheek to his. "We should have sung a number together too! I never even thought of it until it was too late!"

"I'd like you to meet a friend of mine, Wen—Wesli," he corrected himself. He turned to include Ellie. "This is Ellie Nee. Ellie, Wesli Forano."

"Hello, Ellie. Thank you for loaning us Gabe for the evening. I hope you enjoyed the concert."

Ellie was not given time to respond as requests for "Miss Forano!" caused Wendy to turn her head and acknowledge whoever called her. She turned back briefly to Gabe.

"I wish I had more time, Gabe. Talk to Len. Maybe the four of us or all of us can run out to get a bite to eat. I'm famished! I never eat before a performance."

"Miss Forano!" The voice behind a flashing camera became more insistent.

"I've got to go. Maybe later. . . !" she said, giving Gabe's hand a squeeze, but turning from them just as quickly. She called over her shoulder, "Nice meeting you, Ellie!" and she was gone. Gabe turned to talk to Ellie, but the bandleader came up to them.

"Hollowell!" he called. He extended his hand to Gabe, ignoring Ellie. "Great job, preacher! If you're ever in need of a job tickling the ivories, be sure to give Len or me a call. Hey, listen," he said, lowering his voice and pulling Gabe into his confidence. "Len said to tell you he's sorry, but we've got to jump on a plane right away. Here's a hundred bucks to get yourselves something to eat. The limo and hotel are all taken care of. The check for your time is in the mail. Thanks again; it was a real gig!" He slapped a hundred-dollar bill into Gabe's hand and was gone.

Gabe looked at Ellie, who returned his look with something akin to incredulity on her face. He once again took her arm and they left the loud, crowded backstage area. They did not speak until after they had been driven back to the hotel, changed their clothes, and gotten into Gabe's car. He tried to tip the man who brought his car around, but he was brushed off.

"Mr. Forester took care of everything, Mr. Hollowell. Have a nice evening."

Gabe drove in silence for a few seconds before trusting himself to speak. Ellie was looking straight ahead and he couldn't read her expression. He exhaled slowly before speaking.

"Would you like to stop for something to eat? Len Forester must have thought we were really hungry!" He tried to chuckle, but the effort strangled in his throat.

"No, Gabe, thank you. I ate there before the performance. But I don't think you had opportunity to eat anything. Want to stop somewhere? I could use a cup of coffee."

"I really don't have any appetite, but coffee sounds good." He turned into the first strip mall they passed and found a specialty coffee shop. "Looks like I'll be able to spend the entire one hundred dollars on coffee here," Gabe quipped. They parked, went into the restaurant, and ordered their coffee. Once at the table, Ellie's eyes met Gabe's again.

"This was an emotionally draining evening for you," she said without preamble, her raspy voice softened by her almost-whispered statement. Gabe returned her intense gaze and looked down to stir his coffee. "And I am not speaking of the performance," she added.

"You're right about that, Ellie," he replied. He drank some coffee before continuing. "Wendy and I once planned on marrying. We were young, we were in love. We both loved the theater and music. Things changed—no, *I* changed—and we went our separate ways. Wendy to Broadway and me into the ministry. I didn't know what to think when she called about this performance tonight. I thought we would have time to reminisce, talk about old times. . ."

"Ignite old flames?" she asked bluntly, but not harshly. Their eyes locked and Gabe felt some of the tension loosening. He smiled a sad smile of resignation.

"I suppose that thought had crossed my mind in the past week or so," he admitted. "But deep down I knew it wasn't realistic. But tonight was. . .tough." He leaned back, focusing on his coffee mug. "I had at least wanted to *talk* to her. Find out how Wendy—not Wesli—is really doing. Find out if this is all she'd hoped for. If she's happy. If she's even thought about things of import—her soul, her standing before God. . ." He shook his head. "I wasn't given time to tell her how beautifully she sang, or how wonderful she looked. . .nothing. I don't think I said six words to her in the course of the day!"

"I'm sorry," Ellie said simply. And Gabe knew she was.

"What did you think of the concert?" he asked, glad to have said what was weighing on him and being done with it for the moment.

"She was all you and Donna had told me she was. I was in awe of how glamorous she was until I heard her sing! It was her wonderful way of. . .not just singing, but making the words and music take on beauty and color that was so compelling! I can readily see why she is a professional."

Gabe nodded his agreement. "She has a voice like butter one minute and like a rousing trumpet the next! She really is remarkably talented and gifted." He decided to do some prying of his own for once. "You looked like you were crying at the end of her performance. What was it? Was it that final song?"

Ellie looked down before answering. "You should have seen me during that 'Wishing' song. I almost had to leave the room. I was crying like a baby!" Gabe gave her time to respond and noted her lips trembled slightly as she began to explain.

"It was so beautiful, the melody so haunting. All my young life I dreamed of being a singer. I too was wonderfully gifted with a marvelous voice. When my family would come home on furlough, it was often embarrassing for my parents. People would rather hear that 'little Chinese African girl sing' than hear what my parents had to say about their labor of love in Kenya. Even in Kenya I was a novelty, often singing in church. Sometimes I would sing at open-air meetings to draw people to hear my father speak. Until the fire." She stopped speaking in her rasping voice and Gabe realized he was holding his breath.

"The fire ended it all. I was less distraught about my disfigurement—although that gave me reason for a lot of pain as a young girl and teenager—than the loss of my voice. I was so angry! So despairing! How could God do this to me? I had sung for Him for all of my eight years! How could he take away my most beautiful treasure?" She stopped, took a breath, but did not wipe at the tears that formed in her eyes, making her long lashes glisten.

"So, I poured myself into making music with an instrument—any instrument I could play with the restrictions imposed by the burns to my right hand and arm. I excelled in the cello and used that talent to help pay my way through college. But *my* instrument," she touched her scarred hand to her throat, "was gone. And it was a long time before I let go of my anger, but with God's help, I did. And," she said, now wiping away the tears, "as I told you before, the Lord healed me of my anger over my loss. But sometimes, like tonight, one cannot help but feel saddened to think again of what might have been. I would so love to be able to sing again. . ." She smiled an embarrassed smile. "You've just heard more than anyone else ever has about this subject. Yet there is something therapeutic in shared disappointment. So, I've shared mine with you." They both looked down briefly, but Ellie's next words caused Gabe to look up.

"But someday, I shall sing again!" she said triumphantly. "And the gracious, kind Father of all will forgive me my times of tears, of anger, and of wistful imaginings." She became pensive again and reached to touch Gabe's arm across the table. "And so He has done and will do for you, Gabriel. It is not wrong to wonder about what might have been. But we must not dwell on it to the exclusion of what *is*. God has given me grace about my loss of voice and flawless skin. He will do the same for you where Wendy is concerned."

Gabe was again conscious of Ellie, just as he had been before the benefit concert. He entwined the fingers of his free hand around hers. She did not pull her hand away, but responded with a look of tenderness and expectation.

"I know He will," he agreed. *And He already is!* he thought with no small degree of amazement.

When Gabe Hollowell and Ellie Nee walked to Gabe's car an hour later, they were still holding hands. And at church the next morning, it was only the meticulous Donna who saw the briefest special smile that Gabe and Ellie exchanged as they took their respective places at the piano and cello to play a duet for the offertory. Donna mumbled to herself, shaking her head in resignation.

"I can tell," she muttered, "that the organization of the music ministry here is about to take another hit!"

But she was smiling when she said it.

CHAPTER 12

Coming Home

God sets the lonely in families. . .
—Psalm 68:6 NIV

This has been the longest flight of my life!" Paige Zimmerman shook her head. "No, make that the second longest. Flying down here to pick up Anna was the longest."

She shifted uncomfortably in the jet that was carrying her, her husband, and their newly adopted daughter back home to their native Minnesota. She looked again at Peter who gently cradled Anna Meredith in his muscular arms. She smiled at her husband who traced the longest, blackest eyelashes he had ever seen with the lightest touch of his finger.

"You're a natural, Daddy," she said. "You look like you've been doing that all your life."

"Can you believe it, Paige? We have a daughter! And she is more beautiful than either of the two pictures they sent us! The Lord has given us a little girl! She's perfect!"

"I hope you'll still be saying that when she's up all night with a cold—or when she's fifteen and has an attitude!" Paige reached over to touch her finger to Anna's perfectly shaped lips. "But I couldn't agree with you more," she said quietly. "And I don't care if she keeps me up at night. We finally have a child! Eight years of marriage and now we're a bona fide family." Paige giggled happily as Anna began sucking almost imperceptibly.

"Do you think we should have told our families? I'm wondering now if we should just drop by my folks' place or yours with our surprise: 'There's something we've been meaning to tell you. You have a new granddaughter.' " Peter voiced his doubt about the wisdom of their secrecy. Perhaps they should have told their parents about the finally realized adoption.

Paige leaned back in her seat again, content to simply watch Anna's rhythmic breathing. "I don't know. I've been mulling it over myself, to tell you the truth. But after we've had so many 'almosts,' I couldn't stand the thought of putting them through one more emotional upheaval." She scratched her head briefly. "What I've grappled with more is believing Rae managed to keep it a secret! Before we left Wednesday she was quite emphatic that she hadn't 'accidentally let it slip' to anyone."

"Need I remind you that your sister has never kept a secret in her life?" Peter turned his attention away from Anna briefly to give his wife a skeptical smile.

"No, you don't. But I think she managed it this time. At least, that's what I'm banking on!" Paige wanted to hold Anna again, but could see Peter was savoring every second in his new role as a father. His delight gave her joy and she contented herself with stroking Anna's loosely clasped fist. She again secretly thanked God for their answered prayer. "I want to have Anna all to ourselves in our own house for a day or two," she continued. "Then we can call the folks and siblings to come and celebrate with us. I stocked the refrigerator in anticipation of a welcome home party for Anna when we're ready. Maybe we can have one tomorrow or the next day."

"Don't forget the great-grandparents. Your grandmother and my Grandpa Albert would like nothing better than to have an excuse to size each other up again."

"Weren't they something at Christmas? I wasn't sure if they were attracted to each other or looking for a fight! I don't know, darling," she said with a shake of her head. "I don't think we should ever have our two families together again. It's a volatile situation at best."

Peter nodded his head in agreement. "Rachel and Mari about locked horns at Christmas too. My two brothers can hardly speak three civil words to each other—even without your family around! And our mothers tend to get a little testy with each other. Funny," he mused, "I don't remember all that tension at our wedding! Of course, that's been a while back and all my concentration was on my beautiful new bride."

His gray-blue eyes twinkled as he touched a finger to the tip of her nose, something he had done since their college days. Paige never tired of it. It was part of his private language of love with her. She quickly jerked her head up to bite his finger, but their well-played game had shown Peter to have the quicker reflexes. She almost always missed his finger, just as she did now. His grin was small, but triumphant.

"Be all that as it may," she said, their brief game at an end, "sooner or later everyone in the family is going to want to get a good look at this lovely young lady. I'm afraid we'll have a hard time keeping her to ourselves! We'll just have to spread out their introductory visits as well as we can."

"Let's try to keep our secret two more days. That will take us to Monday, since today is Saturday. You know the descent of the Pauldings and the Zimmermans will leave us exhausted and cranky once they all begin to come. Frank and Marshall will cover for me at the office the first few days of the week. Mario will handle all the surgeries." Peter turned his full attention back to Anna, who began to stretch in his arms.

"You've got yourself a deal, Dr. Zimmerman," Paige answered. She rested her head on Peter's shoulder to gaze at Anna as he did. "It will be just the three of us for two more wonderful days!"

"SURPRISE!"

The onslaught of relatives—not just immediate family, but aunts, uncles, cousins, and more—yelling and jumping from behind doors and chairs, stunned Peter and Paige as they entered their house. For her part, the sleepy Anna responded with a startled scream.

"Let me see her!"

"How could you keep such a wonderful secret from us?"

"Our first granddaughter!"

"Why didn't you tell us?"

"Get out of the way of the camera!"

"Let me see, Uncle Peter!"

"She's MY niece, Darcy. I should go first!"

"Oh! You've all gone and scared her!" Paige's mother said in rebuke.

"Oh, isn't she just precious, Jacqueline? Look at those eyelashes!" cooed Peter's mother, Dorothy, with a reach for the bawling bundle in Paige's arms.

Eager hands reached out towards the new arrival and Paige found herself and Anna crushed by enthusiastic, well-meaning family members who crowded for a look or touch. Paige was overwhelmed and speechless; Anna was overwhelmed and screaming.

"You're blocking the video, Jackie! Get over to the right!" Paige's father, Russell, shouted impatiently.

"Dorothy, get her and hold her up for the camera!" Chuck

ordered his wife from atop a dining room chair. He wielded his 35 mm camera, complete with flash and telephoto lens, to challenge Russell's video camera.

Paige looked to Peter for help over Anna's head, but he had been lost to her immediate sight behind backslapping brothers. He was still struggling with his hands and arms full of suitcases, his briefcase, and a new diaper bag. Anna was still bellowing. Paige was still dumbstruck.

"EVERYBODY BACK OFF A MINUTE!"

Even Anna halted her tearful wail at the roared command. Paige took the split second to calm Anna against her shoulder with gentle hushes and patting. The next few seconds were controlled chaos as Rachel, Paige's eldest sister and an army lieutenant, took charge. She commandeered Paige and the more quietly crying Anna to the family room sofa, while keeping eager family members at bay. She half-coaxed, half-jerked Peter to Paige's side, roughly ordering Peter's youngest brother to take care of the luggage and to "Close that door before we all catch pneumonia, buzzard brain!"

In a few brief minutes some semblance of order was again achieved. Anna's wailing had dropped to a wide-eyed whimper and Peter's older brother, Chuck Jr., had shooed the younger children down to the basement. Rachel helped Paige remove her coat so she could remove Anna's blankets, hat, and snowsuit.

"Now, all of you—including you grandmas and grandpas—just stay back a minute more for a few family pictures on Anna's first day home," Rachel said over her shoulder. "And then in an *orderly* manner come up and take turns holding the newest member of the Paulding and Zimmerman clans. Grandmas and grandpas first, of course."

"All right!" exuded Peter's youngest brother, who could see no reason for all this hullabaloo over a baby. He went to turn on the football game.

"Hey, Jake! Turn on the news channel, will ya? I want to see what's happening with that latest mess in Afghanistan."

"You want the news, read the newspaper, Charlie. I'm turning on the game!"

Peter was just about to get up and make sure the dispute didn't go further when his mother-in-law grabbed his arm.

"Why didn't you tell us, Pete?" Jackie asked. "Did you think you could keep this kind of thing under wraps until she went to kindergarten?"

Paige cringed. *He* hates *being called Pete.*

"We just thought that—" Peter tried to answer.

"Drop it, Jackie. The kids would have told us soon enough!" Russ interrupted, dismissing his wife's question. He looked apologetically at his son-in-law. "Don't pay your whining mother-in-law any attention, Peter. She's just miffed she couldn't brag up her new grandbaby before now."

"You know that thing is recording everything you say, don't you, Russ?" Chuck Sr. asked. "You need one of these," he said, holding up his 35 mm camera. "No incriminating microphone!" Both men laughed.

"You got a point there, Chuck!"

"Oh, let me see her, Paige," Jackie reached again for her new granddaughter, who had finally stopped crying and appeared to be in a state of mingled perplexity and amusement. She reached for one of Jackie's large, gold earrings. Paige turned over her daughter to her mother.

"Look, Dot—isn't she the sweetest thing?" She turned to hold Anna towards Dorothy, who managed to wedge her generous frame between Jackie and Peter. In silent, mutual agreement, Peter and Paige both got up from the sofa and let the assorted, eager family members scoot in and around the grandmothers, including the new grandfathers, who still were competing for the best shot and ordering everyone else out of the way.

Peter went to make sure some sort of truce had been reached over the television thing between his two brothers. It didn't take much to ignite a skirmish between them. Meanwhile, Paige grabbed Rachel's arm and steered her into the kitchen.

"What happened to our secret, Rae? I thought you told us—"

"I told you that I didn't let it slip *accidentally*," Rachel said, not giving Paige her full attention, but giving hard looks and making threatening gestures to the excited younger children in the next room. She could see at least three of them right in Anna's face. "No," she continued, still not looking at Paige, "I just out and out told everyone point-blank! A wonderful event like this should never be—ZACH ZIMMERMAN! Get that obnoxious racket-maker away from the baby's ears! She'll go deaf in two minutes!" Rachel yelled, oblivious that her shrill shriek could easily accomplish the same. She charged back into the adjoining room for young Zachary. Zach was quicker, however. He laughed and made a mad dash down the stairs to the basement before she could reach him.

"Aunt Paige?" asked a little voice from somewhere near Paige's knee. She knelt down to look her youngest niece in the eyes.

"Yes, sweetheart? What is it?"

"Do you have some games I could play?"

"Don't bother your auntie now, Bess. Go down to the basement with the rest of the kids." Mari, Peter's sister, directed her daughter to the basement with one hand and turned back to Paige in the next breath. "Aren't you excited, Paige? How long have you had her?"

"We picked her up at the airport in Chicago Friday morning."

"And what's her full name again and where did you get her from?"

"Anna Meredith. She's from Korea."

"Well. That explains why she doesn't look like either of you. You'd think those agencies could do a better job lining up kids with adults as far as looks. It will be obvious to everyone she's adopted."

"Who cares about that? The important thing is—"

"Margret, leave your sister alone!" Mari corrected, turning abruptly from Paige.

Paige's ready defense of Anna and her adoption were lost to her sister-in-law, who was busy now with two of her own children. She counted to ten, prayed away her sharp retort, and went to make some coffee. Someone had already made it, so she poured herself a cup. *Mari didn't know any better,* Paige consoled herself. She got pregnant if she and her husband used the same drinking glass. She hadn't had to go the route of fertility testing, adoption agencies, home inspections. . .

"There you are, dear!"

Paige turned to face her grandmother, a rather morose, but active, seventy-something former teacher. "Grandma! I didn't know you were here too!" Paige returned her gentle hug and kiss. "Have you seen Anna Meredith yet?"

"Oh no, but I will. I don't think she'll be walking off to kindergarten today! May I have a cup?" she asked.

Paige poured her a cup and was just about to catch up on all the news from her former hometown when Peter's grandfather, Albert, walked in. He looked like a bulldog to Paige: short, solidly built, but tilting towards obesity, with jowls that begged to be pinched. Peter had inherited his gray-blue eyes. Fortunately, he hadn't inherited his disposition. Paige found him gruff, at best. Peter once told her he used to be a lively conversationalist. But when his wife died, his talkative, gentle grandfather underwent a transformation. His jovial banter was rare since then, Peter said, and so Paige had never gotten to meet the Albert Zimmerman that Peter had known most of his life.

"Hello, Paige. Ernestine." He gave Paige a half-hug. He gave her grandmother a stiff nod. "Nice to see you again," his tone to Ernestine a denial of the words he spoke.

"Sure it is," Ernestine retorted. "Haven't you got anything better to do than lie through those false teeth of yours, Albert Zimmerman?" She abruptly turned on her heel and left the kitchen, leaving her cup of coffee untouched. Paige was mortified.

"I. . .uh. . .would you like some coffee, Albert?" she asked. She had never seen anyone—especially her grandmother—speak so rudely to anyone! The older man astonished her further when he snickered, quickly pouring himself some coffee.

"That old biddy's got some spunk, I tell you. I *like* that in a woman!" He picked up Ernestine's cup of coffee along with his own and followed Paige's grandmother out of the kitchen without a backward glance at Paige.

"Has one baby made everyone in this house crazy?" she muttered, completely mystified by the exchange she had just witnessed.

Rachel came charging back into the kitchen all business.

"Now don't you worry about anything out here, Paige. You had plenty of food and Mom and I made up some hot chicken for sandwiches. You had better get in there to field questions about Annie."

Anna, Paige corrected, but she kept it to herself. She swallowed the last of her coffee and filled a cup to take to Peter. There was still a mob around Anna, cooing and giggling. It brought a smile to Paige's face, in spite of all the commotion.

Anna looked content enough, so Paige went to look for Peter. She found him setting up a game of table tennis in the basement for the assortment of nieces and nephews present. They had quickly tired of their new cousin.

"Coffee?" she asked, holding the cup out to him.

"There! All done, kids. Have at it!" He took the coffee from Paige with a wink and a grateful smile. They quickly moved away from the table, suddenly surrounded as it was with three of the boys and one of the girls.

"This wasn't the quiet homecoming I had planned on," he whispered.

"I'm sorry, honey. Rae did this. On purpose. Do you think she's trying to get even with me for setting her up on that blind date with the seminary student? I thought he seemed like a nice guy." They climbed the stairs together. She smiled as she remembered what Peter had said, *The guy was a dweeb, Paige.*

"I doubt it. Just her way to let everyone in on the good news at once. I just wish," Peter said, still whispering, "she'd done this at *her* house!"

"There you are, you two! Come, come! We still need a first family picture," Chuck Sr. called out when he saw them.

There was some shifting (and shoving) and nudging (and elbowing), but finally Peter, Paige, Anna, Russell and Jackie, Chuck and Dorothy, the glaring Ernestine and the chortling Albert were arranged semi-comfortably on and around the sofa. It took an additional few minutes to coax Chuck Jr. down from the upstairs television to take the photograph.

"I don't remember all this hoopla when Charles Zimmerman the third came home!" he said good-naturedly.

"That's because Charles Zimmerman the third wasn't flown in from Seoul, Korea, Charlie Z!" Peter reminded his brother.

"No, I only went through eighteen hours of hard labor for

him and then ended up being cut from stem to stern anyway!" Chuck's wife, Nora, put in. "There's no justice!"

"Okay, smiles, everyone! You too, Gran'pap. You look like Winston Churchill on a bad day."

"Winston Churchill was a great man, Charles Zimmerman! You watch what you say!" piped up Ernestine. "And don't be comparing your grandfather with that great man."

"Just take the picture, Dad!" Peter groaned, rubbing his leg which was nearly hidden under his mother's bulk. She leaned over him to straighten the new dress she had somehow managed to get on Anna. The magenta and white dress made her look like a giant turnip with a bewildered face.

Who would buy that kind of getup for a baby? Paige mused. *I wonder if Dorothy dressed Peter up to look like some kind of vegetable when he was a baby.*

"Okay! SMILE!"

The flash set Anna off into a fresh round of terrified screaming and Paige wasn't too far behind her, ready to do the same.

"Time to eat, everyone!" Rachel called from the kitchen. The stampede from the basement temporarily flustered Rachel. But only temporarily. "Adults FIRST, you bunch of morons!"

Can't you do something about your sister's charming appellations? said Peter's frustrated look. Paige was rubbing her forehead. Her older sister had all the finesse of a drill sergeant.

Maybe that's why she's a lieutenant, she reasoned.

"I need to change Anna," she said, getting up as quickly as she could with the crying baby and heading towards the nursery.

"Oh, let me do it, dear," offered her mother, but Paige pretended temporary deafness and went up the stairs quickly. When she reached Anna's room, she quietly shut the door to drown out the cacophony from downstairs. Anna stopped crying and took in the room with alert, bright eyes. Her tears did not prevent her from seeing the colorful mobile above her changing table. It immediately had her attention.

"Lord, will we survive this afternoon?" Paige asked aloud. She touched her nose to Anna's and began humming. Either she was already becoming an overprotective mother, or their two families were getting more bizarre by the day. Or both. She lifted Anna after the diaper change and walked toward the rocker.

"May I?" Albert stuck his head in the door.

"Come in, Grandpa Zimmerman. Would you like to rock Anna for a while? I think the excitement has about done her in." She only hoped Anna wouldn't take one look at her great-grandpa and start shrieking again.

"Not to mention you," he said, sitting down in the rocking chair and holding out his bulldog arms for his new great-granddaughter.

That's about the most sensitive, nice thing he's ever said to me! Paige reflected.

He began rocking Anna and cooing. She in turn reached up for his glasses. Paige couldn't believe her eyes or ears. This must be a side of Albert Zimmerman no one in the entire world had ever seen! Anna smiled widely at him. And he smiled back!

"Oh! I thought you were in here alone with the baby, Paige." Paige's grandmother stood at the door.

"Come on in, Grandma," Paige invited. She motioned for Ernestine to sit on the small love seat by the window.

"That's all right. I'll see her up close later." Ernestine started to exit.

"Come on, Ernestine," coaxed Albert. "We'll take turns spoiling her. I promise not to make one ornery remark about your purple hair of last Christmas." Ernestine looked like she would jump into a war of words with Albert right then, but suddenly she laughed.

"It was pretty atrocious, wasn't it, Albert?"

"I wouldn't be the one to say it, Ernestine. But your hair looks like white silk. Why did you color it anyway? It accents your beautiful, hazel. . .Paige, don't you have some guests to return to?" he abruptly asked Paige.

Paige realized she was standing with her mouth hanging open at this exchange and made some hurried excuse to exit the room.

"We'll be down shortly," her grandmother called softly after her.

As Paige reached the hallway, she heard her grandmother speak in a sweet, buttery voice. "Now, tell me again what you started to say about my hair and eyes, Albert Zimmerman."

"Please call me 'Bert,' Ernestine. . ."

"Very well, *Bert*. You were saying. . . ?"

Paige went back downstairs and sat next to her sister-in-law, Mari, in a near stupor. Had Rachel put some secret military ingredient into the coffee? Was she hallucinating? Weren't her grandmother and Peter's grandfather just. . . ?

"Paige? You didn't hear a word I just said!"

Paige startled and focused on Mari. "I'm sorry. . .what? What did you say?"

"I asked if Annie is okay. Is there anything physically the matter with her?"

Why fight it? She sighed. " 'Annie' is as healthy as she can be. She does have bilateral clubbed feet, but that can be remedied," she answered.

"Good thing you're married to an orthopedist. Did you know about it before you got her?"

"Yes, we did."

"There you are, sis! Congratulations! Sorry to be late—Rae let me in on the secret early, but I couldn't get the day off. Hi,

Mari. How are you?"

"You remember my sister, Paula, don't you, Mari?" Paige asked.

"Sure. Hello again, Paula. Here, you can have my seat—I need to check on Bess and her brothers." Mari excused herself.

"I did get to see Anna before you had your sandwich picture taken. (I can't believe you could fit anyone else on the couch other than Dot! You guys were smashed like sardines in a can!) She is precious, Paige. She doesn't look like either of you, however."

Here we go again. . . !

"She's Korean, Paula. How could she look like us? We don't have a drop of Korean blood in our veins!"

"Did you try to get a Caucasian child?"

If Mari and Paula had said the same thing with anything other than childlike candor, Paige would have thrown them both out of the house. She prayed again to be more charitable and smiled as big a smile as she could muster. Which wasn't much.

"Yes, Paula. Caucasian, Asian, Black, Indian; we aren't picky. We're both over thirty. The biological clock is ticking!"

"Well," Paula said, pulling her into a quick hug, "we're all thrilled for you."

"Paige!" Peter's mother came waddling over to her daughter-in-law. "Your mother and I were just talking. We don't think there are any Annas or Maribels. . ."

"Meredith," Paige interjected.

"Whatever. . .in either family. Where did you get her name?"

"Out of a book, Mother Zimmerman," she answered simply.

"But. . .but why?" Dorothy asked, gesturing with her hands in confused frustration.

"Because we liked the names," Paige explained.

Her mother-in-law thought on that for a moment. "Strange," she murmured, walking away. Paula and Paige looked at each other and stifled their giggles.

" 'Strange' is right!" Paula whispered. "How did Peter end up normal?"

"Pete! Did you notice that the baby's feet look odd?" Jackie asked her son-in-law.

"She has equinus varus, Jackie. Clubbed feet. She'll have to have surgery." *Maybe I should call Frank and tell him I'll take calls for the next few hours. It might get me out of this madhouse!*

"Does that mean she won't be able to run track? Paige was a runner in high school and college, you know."

"Yes, Jackie, I know. Don't worry about it; it will be fine. Excuse me a minute, would you? I think my brothers need me." He backed away from his mother-in-law and went to the living room.

Rachel stopped him before he got to the living room. "Peter!"

"Yes, Rae?" he asked. She took his arm and uncharacteristically lowered her voice.

"I hope you and Paige don't mind the surprise homecoming party. I just thought it would be such a good excuse to get the families together again and then free you two—I mean, three —to get all organized. We'll have the two of you open all the gifts in a little bit and then have some cake before sending everyone on his or her way. Be honest now. Don't you think this was a great way to get the Zimmermans and Pauldings together again? Your family and ours just seem to hit it off so well!"

"You really think so?" he asked, shocked that anyone would think that. The house was a powder keg of Type A personalities and "my way or the highway" opinionated extroverts!

"GET AWAY FROM THAT CAKE, JACOB ZIMMER-MAN, OR I'LL KNOCK YOUR BLOCK OFF!" Rachel stomped over to where Jake was just licking the evidence off his fingers.

"Case in point," Peter murmured as he went to get a second cup of coffee and something for a headache.

That was how the entire afternoon went. By the time everyone had left, Rachel and Paula had cleaned up, picked up, and straightened up the whole house for Paige. Peter, Paige, and their daughter finally sat alone in their family room, *comfortably* positioned on the sofa. Anna busily gummed a soft rattle, a gift from one of her grandmothers. Peter was drinking his sixth or seventh cup of coffee (he suspected he wouldn't sleep a wink when it was time to go to bed), and Paige tiredly, but smilingly, looked through all of the gifts one more time.

"Everything is simply wonderful," she sighed, holding up the prize: a quilt for which each of her sisters, sisters-in-law, mothers, and grandmother had stitched a square. She had cried when she opened it; she got misty looking at it now. "This is the most lovely gift I've ever received," she said.

"It is beautifully done," Peter agreed, admiring the handiwork. "And I can't believe the guys all ganging together to put up that swing set just today. Of course, by the time Anna uses it, it may be rusted. That gift may have been a bit premature."

"But so thoughtful," Paige reflected. Peter nodded his head in agreement, leaning down to kiss Anna on the head. He sat back up, stretching his legs out and kicking off his shoes.

"Is it just me, or do we have more than our share of neurotics and obsessive compulsives in our two families?"

Paige laughed quietly, gently putting the quilt aside. "I

don't know if I'd call them that. Kinder, gentler words like. . . tactless, abrasive, and insensitive might be more fitting."

"But you have to love 'em," Peter chuckled.

"I remember hearing someone say once that you can't pick your family," Paige said. She positioned Anna on her lap. She bounced her a few times and looked sidelong at Peter, who had tilted his head back and closed his eyes. "If you could," she asked him, "would you pick another family to grow up in?"

"You mean, never have to separate my at-odds brothers, or act pleased when my overweight mother almost smushes me within my first few days of becoming a father? Or put up with my dad the perfectionist? Or have to discipline my hyperactive, superdestructive nephews?"

"You're exaggerating, Peter," Paige said. He opened one eye to look at her and Paige started giggling. "No, you're not."

"I most certainly am not," he said with as stoic a look as he could muster with both eyes closed again.

"Did your mom dress you like a turnip when you were little?" Paige asked, smoothing the swirling magenta and white dress on Anna.

"You noticed that too, huh?" He paused for effect. "Of course she didn't! She dressed me like a man. Dapper sailor suits or miniature tuxedos with frilly shirts."

"You're kidding."

"I don't joke about the way my mother used to dress me. But at least I don't have a sister who's like a drill sergeant, carrying on like some jungle commando!" He suddenly jumped to his feet, pointing, and barking out rapid-fire commands.

"'GET AWAY FROM THAT CAKE, GRANDMA! YOU'RE DIABETIC! JAKE, TURN OFF THAT TV BEFORE I TURN IT OFF FOR YOU! PAULA, CLEAN UP YOUR KID'S VOMIT BEFORE I CLEAN YOUR CLOCK!'"

Paige laughed hysterically; Anna's puzzled stare darted between her mother and father.

"She was in rare form today, wasn't she?" Paige managed to get out in the midst of her laughter.

" 'Rare form' is an understatement, if ever there was one," Peter said, plopping back down on the sofa. "I can't believe all the windows are still intact."

"Did you happen to catch any of the dialog between Grandma Paulding and your grandfather today?" Paige asked.

"I know he brought her a cup of coffee, which she almost threw on him. In return, he threw some equally charming epithets at her that included words like 'pompous' and 'uppity.' "

"You won't believe what I heard them say in the nursery then," Paige said. "As a matter of fact, I can scarcely believe it myself!"

"Don't tell me it got worse!"

"Just the opposite. I had gone in to. . ."

The doorbell rang, interrupting their discussion. Peter got up to get it. Paige lifted Anna into her arms to follow Peter to the front door. She was surprised to find her grandmother and Peter's grandfather there. Together. Smiling. It was uncanny and unnatural.

It gave her the creeps.

"Hello, dear. . .hello, my precious Anna Meredith," her grandmother said, giving both Paige and Anna a kiss on the cheek. This was the Grandmother Paulding Paige knew—none of that earlier discourtesy in the kitchen episode.

"Hello, Paige. How is my sweet, new great-grandbaby doing?" asked Albert with a winsome smile. That was *not* the Grandfather Zimmerman that Paige knew. She glanced at Peter, who was smiling somewhat incredulously.

"I think I might have dropped an earring in the nursery,

Paige," her grandmother said. "I'll just run up and see if I can find it."

"Let me help you look," Paige offered, handing Anna to Peter.

"No, no, no. I can look for myself. It will only take a minute," she answered, quickly going up the stairs.

Paige turned to Albert, whom she noted was watching Ernestine go up the stairs. Peter raised his eyebrows at Paige in question.

"That grandmother of yours is quite a lady, Paige," the bulldog said. "She's got a sharp tongue, but a sharp wit too. She's quite a student of theology and the Bible too. Do you know she can hold her own in a discussion of Calvinism and Arminianism with me? First woman I ever met who could!"

Before Paige or Peter could respond, Ernestine started back down the stairs. "Found it!" she declared.

"Would you two like to have a cup of coffee or some iced tea?" Paige asked.

"I don't think so, but could I use your phone just a minute?" asked Albert. Peter took him to the other room to show him where the telephone was. As soon as they left the foyer, Ernestine turned to Paige with dancing eyes.

"Isn't he something?" she gushed. "Do you know he and I have the same interests in eschatology and Dixieland jazz?"

Now there's a combination! thought Paige.

"We've been together ever since we left your house," Ernestine continued in an excited whisper. "For all his bluster, he is a gentleman like few I've ever met!"

The men came back into the room. "The planetarium is open tonight, Erni! Let's run over there!"

The two of them pulled their gloves back on, bid their grandchildren and great-granddaughter "good night," and were gone as quickly as they had arrived. They chattered happily to the car, scarcely waving good-bye as Albert opened the passenger door for Ernestine and then quickly went around to the driver's door. They drove off into the chill February night.

The new Zimmerman family went back into their family room, Anna once again chewing contentedly on her teething ring. Peter and Paige sat quietly on the sofa for a few seconds before Peter spoke.

"Did you see and hear what I just saw and heard?" he asked.

Paige did, but she couldn't believe it either. In a four-minute visit their memory of the day's earlier excitement—the eager, welcoming touches, the mayhem, and the cacophony—was already dwindling. Peter looked at his wife, whose merry grin began spreading across her face the same as her husband's. They were thinking the same thing; they could read it in each other's eyes.

"BERT AND ERNI!" they declared together, dissolving into gales of laughter.